SMILEY JUN

*Tom Creighton*

COPENHAGEN WAS THE BEGINNING....

Strange aircraft had been reported in the skies over Denmark—immense and spherical, capable of flying vertically as well as horizontally, and at such high velocities that they were gone almost before they could be spotted by observers.

*Flying saucers?* Perhaps—but flying saucers developed and controlled by THRUSH!

Their purpose? The purpose of THRUSH itself—to subdue and rule all the world's nations.

*THE ENDING COULD ONLY BE DESTRUCTION....*

Don't miss these other full-length adventures in international suspense starring Napoleon Solo and Illya Kuryakin, top enforcement officers for U.N.C.L.E.:

G-553 — 50¢
THE MAN FROM U.N.C.L.E. #1
*The Thousand Coffins Affair* by Michael Avallone

G-560 — 50¢
THE MAN FROM U.N.C.L.E. #2
*The Doomsday Affair* by Harry Whittington

If your newsdealer is out of stock on these books, they may be purchased directly from the publisher by sending 50¢ each, plus 5¢ handling fee, to Ace Books, Inc. (Dept. MM), 1120 Avenue of the Americas, New York, N.Y., 10036.

# THE MAN FROM U.N.C.L.E.

NUMBER **3**

## The Copenhagen Affair

**by John Oram**

Ace Books Inc.
1120 Avenue of the Americas
New York, N.Y. 10036

THE COPENHAGEN AFFAIR

# PROLOGUE

**T**HERE IS A ROW of buildings in New York
City, a few blocks from the United Nations Building.
It consists, starting from the south end, of a three-
storied whitestone which appears fairly new in contrast
with the series of brownstones which make up most of
the row, and at the north end a busy public garage.
The brownstones are occupied by a few lower-income
families living above the decrepit shops and business
premises at street level. Del Floria's tailor shop occupies
the street level space in a brownstone near the middle
of the block. The first and second floors of the whitestone are taken up by an exclusive "key club" restau-
rant named *The Mask Club*, which features fine food
served by waitresses wearing masks (and very little else)
to patrons who don masks covering nostrils to brow as
they enter.

On the third floor of the whitestone is a sedate suite of offices, the entrance to which bears the engraved letters U.N.C.L.E. And in this suite of offices a rather ordinary group of people handle mail, meet and do business with visitors, and in general give the impression of some normal organization engaged in a special charity project or a fund foundation headquarters.

All these buildings are owned by U.N.C.L.E. All the people involved in the activities of the garage and the key-club are in the employ of U.N.C.L.E.; many of the patrons of *The Mask Club* are affiliated with U.N.C.L.E.; and even the frowsy tenants of the brownstones, including old Del Floria, the tailor, are members of the organization.

Behind the outer, crumbling skin of the four old brownstone buildings in the middle of the row is one large edifice comprising three floors of a modern, complex office building . . . a steel maze of corridors and suites containing brisk, alert young people of many races, creeds, colors and national origins . . . as well as complex masses of modern machinery for business and communications.

There are no staircases. Four elevators handle traffic vertically. Below basement level an underground channel has been cut through from the East River, and several cruisers (the largest sixty feet long) are bobbing at the underground wharf beneath the brownstone complex. If you could ascend to the roof and examine the huge neon advertising sign there, you might detect that its supporting pillars concealed a high-powered short-wave aerial and elaborate electronic receiving and transmitting equipment.

# CHAPTER ONE

SOMEHOW, NEAR CHRISTMAS, even the sleek SAS Convair Coronado 990, fastest airliner in the world, seems to take on some of the season's magic.

Cheerful Danish expatriates, arms laden with bright-wrapped packages, crowd aboard, heading home from London for the *Juleaften* feast. There's an extra-welcoming smile on the face of the pretty stewardess and an extra warmth in the cabin after the raw air on the tarmac. Nobody would be much surprised if Santa himself came beaming through the pilot's hatch to greet the hundred passengers.

Christmas spirit? If you are not on the best of terms with your next-seat neighbor by the time you have eaten your smorrebrod and drunk your first glass of Tuborg you must be a Scrooge indeed. The Danes are always friendly, but there's something about a December flight that breaks down the last barriers.

Mike Stanning hoped the girl beside him would get the message.

He had noticed her first in the departure lounge at the airport. She had been sitting alone—a slim, trim figure in neat, expensive tweeds. She wore no hat. Black,

9

shoulder-length hair framed her oval face like a glossy helmet. The hand turning and re-turning the untasted glass on the table before her was brown, well-shaped, with long, sensitive fingers. When she had stood up at the loudspeaker's summons Mike had seen that she was not more than five feet two but built with the grace of a ballet dancer. He'd taken particular pains to get the seat beside her in the aircraft.

As soon as they had unfastened their seat belts he offered her a cigarette. She shook her head.

He tried her with his inexpert Danish. She said, "I'm sorry. I don't understand." Her voice was low and musical.

Mike said, "Don't worry. The Danes don't understand it, either. But I'm working on it. This is your first time for Copenhagen?"

"Yes."

"Visiting friends?"

"Not exactly."

"Business?" Mike tried again. "I'm in engineering, myself. Salesman, you know. Boost the exports, and all that jazz."

"Yes," she said slowly. "I suppose you could say I was on business." There was a curious expression in her brown eyes. Her tone forbade further questioning. She took up a magazine and began to read.

Mike called the stewardess and ordered a large Scotch. The girl refused a drink. Through the rest of the hour-long flight he tried to interest himself in a paperback novel.

Mike always enjoyed the moment of arrival at Kastrup, surely the friendliest airport anywhere—the waving and smiling of the "reception committees" beyond the barrier as the passengers filed through passport inspection; the hugging and hand-shaking, the kissing and laughter (and not a few tears) as families were reunited.

There was nobody to meet the girl, he noticed. Carrying only a sling-bag of the type they sell in airport gift shops, she pushed quickly through the crowd around the barrier. She did not reappear on the bus for the short trip to the city terminal. Sharing vicariously the excitment around him, Mike forgot about her. He walked out into the bustle of Vesterbrogade, Copenhagen's main street, with a sense of homecoming.

He checked in at the *Excelsior* on the corner of Colbjornsensgade, a modest hotel where the food is excellent even by Copenhagen's exacting standards and the rooms both comfortable and quiet.

"You will be with us for Christmas, Mr. Stanning?" the desk clerk asked.

"No, worse luck. I'll make it someday, but this time it's just a quick trip. I have to be in London in three days' time."

"A pity," the clerk smiled. "There is so little to do here out of season."

"Oh, I don't know," Mike said. "You can usually find a little action around if you care to look for it."

That turned out to be the understatement of his life.

It was while walking through Stroget late the following afternoon that he saw the girl again.

You won't find Stroget on any Copenhagen street map. It is not one street, but five—Ostergade, Amagertorv, Vimmelskatet, Nygade and Frederiksberggade—winding from Kongens Nytorv to the Town Hall Square, where in December the seventy-foot Christmas tree from Grib Skov towers like the presiding genius of the festival.

Think of Piccadilly, Bond Street and Fifth Avenue rolled into one. That's Stroget. You can buy anything along its winding length: furs, trinkets, porcelain, gold and silver, furniture, pictures, antiques, or just a simple toy for a couple of kroner. And in December the sellers of Christmas trees and the *Jul* straw goats are out in force on the sidewalks, their colorful stalls adding to the general gaiety.

There is no traffic problem in Stroget. It has long been closed to all traffic on wheels except baby carriages. So you can stroll along at leisure, crossing from side to side of the street without risk to life or limb. Oddly, this security takes some getting used to. You can always pick out an Englishman or an American by the way he stays grimly on the sidewalk while the Danes parade happily along the middle of the road.

The girl was no exception. She was walking slowly, stopping every now and then to look at the superb window displays.

"Good evening," Mike greeted her. "Just sight-seeing, or is there something you want to buy? I know all the right places."

She smiled up at him. "I'm just idling," she admitted, "and I was getting a little bored with my own company. Would you like to buy me a coffee somewhere?"

"I'll do better," Mike said. "Ever tasted Yule punch? No? Then your education is going to start right now. It's a hot, spiced nectar that every good Dane drinks at Christmas, and I know a little bar that's got the recipe dead to rights." He grinned. "By the way, do you realize I don't even know your name?"

12

"I'm sorry. It's Bland. Norah Bland."

"Nice! And I'm Stanning. Mike Stanning. Like the song says: Lovely to know you."

The next few hours were to live long in Mike's memory.

They were lingering over coffee after a long, late dinner in the Japanese room at *The Seven Nations* when Norah said suddenly, "Will you take me to a place called *The Linden Tree*?"

He looked at her, astonished. "The *Linden?* I thought you said you didn't know Copenhagen."

"I don't."

"Then how do you know about the *Linden?* It's not the sort of joint that attracts the tourist trade."

"It doesn't matter how I know. I just want to go there —now."

He sighed. "Sweetheart," he said, "it's time you heard some of the facts of life. The *Linden* is a rough, tough joint in the heart of Nyhavn, and Nyhavn is the roughest, toughest part of Copenhagen. It's the seamen's quarter, and at this time of night—in case you're not aware of the fact, it's pushing midnight—it's liable to be really jumping. Not that the *Linden* is a spot for well-brought up young women at any time of day. So let's forget it. We'll go to Vingaarden and hear some good jazz."

She said: "Please, Mike—the *Linden Tree*. Now."

He signaled to the waiter. "All right, if you're set on it. But don't blame me if you get your bag snatched—or," he added thoughtfully, "if I get my skull cracked and you have to walk home."

The glaring neons over the bars along Nyhavn were

13

reflected in the black water of the harbor like blood. A party of carousing Swedes stumbled unsteadily along the sidewalk, arguing loudly. Somewhere away in the shadows a woman was shouting a stream of drunken abuse. As Mike paid off the taxi a sudden gust of cold wind made Norah shiver and pull her coat closer around her.

Mike said, "You're sure you want to go through with it?"

"Yes."

"All right. Then stick close. The boys may get wrong ideas."

He pushed open the swinging doors of *The Linden Tree* and led the way down a flight of uncarpeted stairs. At the bottom a man sat wedged between the wall and a small table. His waistline must have been all of sixty inches and his moon face fell to his shabby shirt collar in a succession of flabby wattles. He tore two paper tickets from a roll and wheezed, "Four kroner."

Norah said, "Let me pay, Mike. You've been shelling out for everything so far."

In her haste to forestall him her fingers slipped and her handbag fell to the floor. Lipstick, compact, and the dozen and one things women carry burst out like a shower. Mike knelt to retrieve them. "That Yule punch!" he said. "I warned you it was potent."

They were turning from the table when the fat man called, "Miss, I think you forget something." He held out a small, flat packet.

"Oh! Thanks," Norah said. "I thought we had picked up everything. You're very kind."

He grunted "Velkom!" uninterestedly and returned to his study of the evening paper.

14

They went on into the club. Surprisingly, it was half empty. Four seamen stood talking over their drinks at the small bar counter. A few couples were dancing to the music of a three-piece combo. In a far corner of the long room a boy and girl who looked like students were being uninhibitedly romantic.

Mike chose a table. A waiter came over and lit the inevitable candle of welcome. Mike ordered two lagers.

Norah looked around. "I thought you said this was a rough place," she said. "It looks pretty harmless to me."

"It warms up," he told her. "It's still fairly early for Nyhavn."

A girl came into the room alone. She wore a black, high-necked sweater and tight black trousers. She was tall and thin, with a pale face that looked undernourished. Her thick hair was blazing red. She walked across to their table and put a hand tentatively on the back of a chair. "May I sit?"

"Help yourself," Mike said. "Would you like a drink?"

"Thank you, no. I buy my own."

She fumbled in a shabby purse and produced three kroner. Without being told, the waiter brought her a Carlsberg. She poured it expertly in the Danish fashion, dropping the beer almost vertically into the glass. She raised the glass, nodded, stared at them with vivid blue eyes, said "Skaal!" then nodded again and drank.

After a few minutes she got up and went over to join the seamen at the bar. Curiously, Mike could have sworn that she gave Norah a glance of understanding as she left the table.

"Want to dance?" Mike suggested.

Norah shook her head. "No," she said. "You were

right. This place bores me, and I think I'm tired. Would you mind taking me home?"

"Of course. The only thing is, I don't know where you live."

"I've got an apartment in Marievej, out in Hellerup. A—a friend lent it to me."

He said nothing, and she smiled. "That's what I like about you, Mike," she said. "You're not the inquisitive type."

Suddenly, in the taxi, she was in his arms. She kissed him almost desperately. "We have so little time," she whispered.

He could feel wetness on his cheek and knew she was crying. He said awkwardly, trying to make light of it, "Oh, come on, now. We've got a couple of days together yet. There's nothing to get upset about."

She drew away. "You don't understand. How could you?"

He said, "I'm beginning to understand that you're in some kind of trouble. What is it? The law?"

"No." She seemed to make up her mind. "Mike, I've got to trust you. Please keep this with you until you get back to London. I'll contact you there—at your office."

She opened her bag and brought out the small oblong package the doorman at *The Linden Tree* had given her. In the intermittent light of the street lights he could see that it was wrapped in white paper and that the ends were sealed with wax.

He grinned. "What is it? Purple hearts?"

Her voice was somber. "It's dynamite."

"As long as it doesn't blow up on me, I'll look after it," he answered, stuffing the package in his pocket. Then he took her in his arms again.

to a pair of massive wrought-iron gates, beyond which a drive wound through banks of well-kept shrubs. The bushes gave Mike a hemmed-in feeling. The light had taken on a greenish tinge and there was a dank taste of rotting leaves in the air. After awhile they came out into the open again. Around and about them was a stretch of park land fringed with trees, and right ahead was the Rodehus. The major stopped to let Mike catch his breath and admire the place.

It was a low, rambling house built in the traditional Danish L-shape but looking as if successive generations had kept adding a shingle here and there and tacking on another room for the unexpected guest. The walls were pink-washed and the windows were flanked by open shutters in a deeper red that matched the roof tiles. A Rolls-Royce could have been driven through the main doors without scratching the paintwork. A velvet lawn swept down to meet the parkland.

They went in by the main entrance and found themselves in a large square hall with a black and white stone flagged floor like a checkerboard. Logs were burning in a fireplace large enough to roast an ox. The flames danced on suits of armor and the trophies of arms which decorated the walls. A broad staircase carpeted in purple led up to the first floor and at its head there was a life-size oil painting of a woman in Elizabethan dress. It was all more like an English castle than a Danish country manor.

"Here we are," said the major. "And before we get down to business I think a drink is indicated. Come into the library."

The library was darker than the hall. There was a nice smell of old leather and good tobacco. The main furnishings were easy chairs, a long chesterfield and a massive table-desk. Books covered most of the walls and the rest of the space was occupied by sporting prints.

"Make yourself comfortable," said the major, indicating the chesterfield drawn up to the fire. He pressed the bell and a second or two later a thickset, surly man appeared in the doorway. He was dressed like a butler but he had ex-pug written all over his cauliflower ears and battered nose. His hands matched his face, with the knuckles pushed back halfway up his wrists.

"You rang, sir?"

"Whisky, Charles," said the major.

"I don't want to be awkward," Mike said, "but if it's all the same to you I'll take beer. It's a bit early for the hard stuff."

"Very wise," the major agreed. "Bring some lager, Charles."

The butler brought the drinks, set them on a table and went out, closing the door carefully behind him.

The major poured himself almost half a tumbler of straight Scotch, said "Cheers!" and tossed it down without a blink. He refilled the glass and stood with his back to the fire, looking at Mike thoughtfully.

Suddenly he said, "And now—touching on Norah Bland . . ."

Mike was so surprised that he almost dropped his beer. To gain time he took a long drink.

Then he repeated slowly, "Bland? Norah Bland? Should I know her?"

"You should," the major said. "She is a beautiful girl, and you spent a great deal of last night with her." He was smiling coldly. The affable squire manner had dropped from him and his yellow eyes were like agates.

Mike sighed. "Nothing like that ever happens to me. You must be thinking of two other people."

The major shook his head, still smiling thinly. "It won't do, Stanning. Let me refresh your memory. You met Miss Bland on the plane from London. You met her again yesterday afternoon and the two of you were together until early this morning. You took her to dinner at *The Seven Nations* and then for a drink at *The Linden Tree*—"

Mike said, "Just supposing you happen to be right, which I don't admit, what in hell has it got to do with you?"

He shrugged. "I thought you ought to know that she is dead."

Something cold clutched at Mike's insides. He remembered honest brown eyes under curled lashes, heard the soft voice saying, "We have so little time." He forgot his act and muttered stupidly, "Norah . . . dead? . . . How?"

The major drank again, watching him. At last he said: "After she left you she was in . . . an accident."

"I don't believe it. It's impossible."

He spread his hands. "That's how it goes, old man." He walked over to the desk and unlocked a drawer. "Somebody always draws the last card." He opened the drawer and rested his hand inside. "But before she died," he continued more slowly, "she handed you a sealed packet."

"So?"

His hand came up fast, gripping a 9mm Luger pistol. "So I want it," he snapped.

The sight of the gun acted like a cold shower. Mike came out of his trance.

"Put that thing away," he said. "It doesn't scare me. I'm damned if I know what you're talking about, anyway. Norah gave me no packet."

"She gave it to you—sometime during the night. Hand it over quickly, please."

Mike kept his eyes on the gun pointed unwaveringly at his middle. He said, "Don't be childish. Suppose you squirt that thing—how do you expect to get away with it? The hotel clerk and the switchboard girl know you phoned me this morning, and I left your number with the desk when I started out. Even a country copper couldn't fail to add it up if I disappear."

"You're not going to disappear," said the major. "I was explaining the mechanism of the pistol to you and forgot the shell in the chamber. Don't you ever read the inquest reports? I can only hope that in your case the necessity for such an interesting ceremony will not arise."

Mike forced a grin. "You've got it all figured out, but it won't get you anyplace. The package is tucked away safely, miles from here."

"You underrate my intelligence. You were followed all morning and your room was searched as soon as you had left to come here. The package is not there, and since you have not been near a post office you must have it with you. For the last time, hand it over."

Mike picked up his glass of beer. "You've been seeing too many movies and they've gone to your head. For some reason you saw fit to put a tail on Norah and me and you seem to be pretty well acquainted with our movements. But about the packet you're all wet. Well, if it amuses you, all right. But you've played cops and robbers with me long enough. Now I'll tell you what I'm going to do. I'm going to finish this drink and then I'm going to walk out of here. And if I've got the packet— as you seem to think—it goes out with me."

He raised the glass and drank. His nonchalance would have delighted a charm-school instructress. It had the reverse effect on the major. He swung from behind the desk and came at him, the gun stuck out threateningly.

That was what Mike had played for. As Garbridge came within range he jerked the glass straight into his face. The major's right hand went up instinctively, and in the same instant Mike kicked him right where it would do the most good. Garbridge screamed, dropped the Luger and fell to the carpet, moaning. His face was grayer than his hair. In his football days Mike had been known as a useful place-kicker. And he wanted that gun.

Footsteps pounded across the hall and Charles crashed through the door. He looked down at his boss and cursed.

Mike beckoned him with the Luger. "Get those hands up and stand by the wall," he ordered. "Now listen:

"I'm a peaceful kind of guy, and when a man invites me to have a drink I don't expect him to pump lead into me by way of an appetizer. It upsets my digestion, and when that happens I tend to get more than a little restive. I will be glad if you will explain that to the major when he is in a mood to listen.

"You can tell him, too, that something stinks around this joint. I don't know what it is, but I intend to find out."

Charles scowled.

"Fine!" Mike scowled back, just to show him he had no monopoly. "One last point. Your boss tells me a friend

23

of mine died today. It occurs to me that maybe she was murdered." The butler's piggy eyes flickered. "It occurs to me further," Mike went on, "that you may have had a hand in it. If that proves to be the case I want you to know that I intend to blast hell out of you with nice filed bullets out of this self-same gun. You'll need a bathtub to plug the hole."

"So 'elp me God . . ."

"I hope so," Mike agreed piously. "Meanwhile, turn your face to the wall."

Charles shuffled around apprehensively and Mike brought the barrel of the Luger sharply down on his skull. He crumpled without a murmur.

Mike tucked the gun into the waistband of his trousers, went into the hall and locked the library door on the outside.

He was not frightened but he was far from happy. He could see that as soon as he left the Rodehus he was in a spot. He had ruined the major for horseback riding for quite some time and assaulted his butler with a lethal weapon for which he had no permit. Garbridge had only to telephone the local police and Mike would have plenty of explaining to do. He could not imagine any rural policeman swallowing the story he had to tell, and he had no witnesses.

On top of mayhem and battery and carrying concealed weapons he still had that package, which might contain anything from heroin to a package of safety pins. Judging from the major's anxiety to get his fingers on it, he did not think it would turn out to be the latter.

He listened. There was no sign of movement in the house. If the major had other servants they had obviously been trained to mind their own business. He took

24

out the girl's parting gift, broke the seals and tore off the paper, revealing a plain brown cardboard box and a folded note.

He looked in the box first. All it contained was an unopened pack of Danish cigarettes. He tipped it into his palm and examined it closely. It was a standard brand and the cellophane wrapper was intact. He swore softly and turned his attention to the note.

That gave him another shock. It was from Norah Bland and it was addressed to him.

*Mike,*

*If you read this it means that I haven't shown up to collect the enclosed which, when we get out of here, I'm going to ask you to hold for me. Don't fool with the cigarettes. Take them personally to U.N.C.L.E. offices, New York—and don't let a soul know you have them. If you're broke, borrow transportation. But for God's sake don't lose a minute. Get going, Mike. And good luck.*

Mike's eyes were giving him trouble by the time he had finished reading. It began to look as if Norah had anticipated becoming a casualty. He remembered the sadness that had been in her eyes even while he had held her close in the taxi.

He wondered when she had found time to write the note. He was fairly certain the doorman in the *Linden Tree* had slipped the package to her. Then he remembered that before leaving the club she had gone to powder her nose and had taken more time than had seemed necessary.

He stood for a minute, holding the note and thinking. Then he stuffed note and box back into his pocket, listened briefly for sounds beyond the library door, and made for the main exit.

Darkness had fallen and he knew he would have considerable difficulty in finding his way back to the highway. He cut diagonally across the lawn and onto the shrub-lined lower drive. It was comparatively easy going there. The problem would be to find the path that led through the beech wood. He wished he had a pocket flashlight.

The entrance gates were still open. As he passed through them he heard voices, and, turning briefly, he saw lights somewhere on the park land. Evidently the major had recovered from his indisposition.

The first fringe of beeches loomed ahead. Mike plunged in among the great trees, running blindly. He had no hope now of finding the path; his one thought was to put as much distance as he could between himself and his pursuers. He had no illusion about what would happen if he fell into the major's hands again.

Low branches whipped at his face as he stumbled along, and he felt the salt taste of blood in his mouth. Once he fell, and the sharp pain that stabbed at his ankle made him cry out. He limped on desperately, and then suddenly he was on the highway.

Car headlights blazed in his face. He heard a girl call, "Stanning! Here!"

He found the open door and fell into the seat beside the driver. The motor accelerated smoothly.

The same voice said, "Now, soon, friend Mike, you shall buy the drink you promised me in the *Linden Tree*."

It was the girl with the red hair.

# CHAPTER THREE

NAPOLEON SOLO and Illya Nickovetch Kuryakin entered Del Floria's tailoring shop together. The old man looked up, smiled fleetingly and pushed a small button on the side of his pressing machine.

The two men walked into the third of the "try-on" cubicles at the rear of the shop. Solo drew the curtain while Illya turned the hook on the back wall. The wall swung open and they walked through to the agents' admissions desk of U.N.C.L.E. The girl on the desk had watched their progress on her closed-circuit television screen. She had the two white badges ready to pin to their lapels. A chemical on her fingers set up a reaction in each badge as she pinned it into place.

It is one of the safeguards of the U.N.C.L.E. setup that any person passing through certain areas of the building will trip an alarm unless he is wearing a badge that has been properly activated. On every desk in the building a small red light begins to flash and a signal is heard beating in a repeating tempo of alarm. Steel doors slide shut throughout the enclave, forming self-contained cells in which to trap the intruder. Therefore it is highly . . . uncomfortable . . . to stray from the prescribed limits within which one's badge is valid.

White badge territory is the third floor. Here are the Policy and Operations offices, interrogation rooms, the armory, and the cubicles occupied by the enforcement agents, the elite of the organization, during their infrequent visits to the home base.

Here, too, is the office of Alexander Waverly, one of the five men of different nationalities who comprise the Policy department of U.N.C.L.E.'s Section I. The only window in the entire U.N.C.L.E. fortress is in Waverly's office. It lends itself to a panoric view of the East River with the United Nations building centered in the frame. It is not known how Waverly enters or leaves his office. He is either there or not there. Some say there is a fifth entrance to the building reserved for the five Policy directors alone. If there is, nobody has ever found it.

Waverly is a lean, dry, pedantic man in his early fifties. He looks and talks like a university professor of the old school. He wears seedy tweed jackets with leather-patched arms, baggy flannel trousers and much-darned sweaters. While he talks he handles pipes incessantly, but he has never been seen to smoke one.

In discussions with his enforcement agents he could be lecturing backward students. He talks around points, hesitating, pausing and often "harrumphing" when he comes to a name. Sometimes he will appear even to forget the name of the man he is talking with. There are many things he appears to forget. Somehow, none of them are important. He may forget the name of an agent, but he won't forget the dangers of the situation into which he is sending him. He may seem to be understating the assignment—but he will have analyzed every aspect very thoroughly before selecting the right man or woman for the job.

When Solo and Illya Kuryakin walked into his office Waverly was sitting alone at the great teak revolving table shaped like a hollow O. Without speaking he motioned them to chairs. Then he flipped a switch and spoke briefly into an inter-office transmitter.

The red-haired girl came into the room with Mike Stanning. She was no longer in the worn black turtleneck and trousers. She wore a brown deerskin jacket, a Danish ski-sweater in bright colored wools and white non-stretch slacks. Her feet were shod in light brogues that looked hand-made.

Waverly did not get up to greet her. He asked, "Well, Karen?"

The girl said, "I don't know that I can add anything to my report. Except that he can keep his mouth shut. I've worked on him all the way from Copenhagen. Nothing. Nothing at all."

"Good!"

There was silence for a moment. Then Mr. Waverly said, "All right, Mr. Stanning. Wait in the next room, will you? There are one or two things I want to discuss with these people."

Mike's long-tried patience gave away.

"Look, what the hell's going on?" he burst out. "Who

are you? I'm a businessman and I ought to be in London. Instead of that I've been shanghaied to New York in an army bomber without even being allowed to make a phone call to my boss. For all I know I'm out of a job already. I've got a right to know what it's all about."

"You have, indeed, my dear fellow." Waverly stood up and ushered him to the door. "And so you shall . . . in just a few moments." He opened the door with old-world courtesy but he shut it as firmly as a jailer.

Mike sat down in the small anteroom and began to turn the pages of a magazine he found on a table. It would have made more sense if it had not been printed in Russian. Still, the pictures were interesting.

Karen put her head around the door. "You can come back now."

The party had rearranged itself in his absence. Waverly was still in the same chair but now Solo and Illya sat on either side of him. Karen took her place beside Solo. She lit a torpedo-shaped cigar that looked as out of place as a hayfork in the hand of Venus.

Waverly went straight to the point. "The girl you knew as Norah Bland gave you a package to bring to me," he told Mike.

"Yes."

"You have it with you?"

Mike took the package from his breast pocket and put it on the table. The teak circle revolved smoothly, bringing the white-wrapped package to Waverly's hand. He said, "Have you any idea what is in it?"

"A pack of North State cigarettes."

"And in the cigarettes?"

"I wouldn't know. I haven't touched them," Mike said. "They could be reefers, for all of mine."

"Then let's find out."

Waverly expertly broke open the cellophane and carefully unfolded the blue North State pack. Twenty white tubes rolled gently onto the table. They looked like any other cigarettes.

Waverly picked one up. He slit the cigarette paper vertically with a blade like a scalpel. Mike saw a tiny container nestling between two short cylinders of tobacco. There was a similar container in each of the nineteen remaining cigarettes.

Waverly swept cellophane, paper and tobacco into a wastebasket. He took one of the metal containers between first finger and thumb and held it up.

"These," he said soberly, "are what Norah Bland died for. You cannot be aware of it, Mr.—er, Stanning—but by completing her mission you have done an incalculable service not only to your country but to the world. I am afraid my inadequate thanks are all you will get for it. When you leave this room you must put the matter out of your mind and never speak of it again.

"And now"—he stood up—"transportation is waiting to take you back to Denmark. You will be in Copenhagen in good time to catch the S.A.S. flight to London on which you booked."

He put out his hand, smiling for the first time. "And by the way, don't worry about losing your job. Your firm has just acquired a contract worth a quarter of a million pounds. That will account for your lost time. The appropriate papers are in your briefcase. You can read them on your journey. I can—er—assure you they are quite genuine."

"But—" Mike began.

Waverly shook his head. "I know, I know. You are

going to tell me you have an account to settle with a man called Garbridge. Believe me, that is quite impossible . . . and unnecessary." His tone was final.

Karen stubbed her cigar in a blue glass ashtray, and rose to her feet. "Come on, Mike. I'll see you out of the building."

When they had gone Solo said, "And what, to quote our late guest, was that all about?"

Waverly walked over to a console near the big picture window. He pressed two buttons on the panel and a motion picture projector and a beaded white screen slid quietly into view. The projector measured not more than five by three by one inches. It could have been a child's toy. The spools on the arms were no larger than a silver dollar.

He broke open one of the containers, removed a roll of sub-miniature film, threaded it on to the spools and into the projector. "Watch!"

The room went dark. The projector motor whirred. Something that looked like a dustbin-lid shot rapidly across the bright oblong of the screen. There was what appeared to be an explosion or a direct hit from a shell. Then the screen was blank again.

The room lights went on again. Waverly opened a second container, threaded a second length of film.

This time it showed a stretch of deserted, wooded countryside that might have been in the English Lake District. Again a dustbin-lid object came into sight. It hovered briefly above a group of birches, then dropped vertically and disappeared. This time there was no explosion.

The third film, taken in slow motion with a telephoto

lens, was practically a repetition of the second. But in closeup it could be seen that the "handle" of the lid-like object was a turret or cockpit. What looked like portholes were clearly visible around the "rim".

Solo said unbelievingly, "UFOs! Flying saucers!"

"Exactly." Waverly was pleased. "And where, do you suppose?"

Illya said, "Since the film came from Denmark, I should think Jutland. The scenery looked typical."

"Exactly," Waverly said again. "No doubt the remainder of the films will give us further data."

He led the way back to the table, pressed the button on the intercom and said, "Bring me File A/D/976."

A pretty Negress hurried in with a bulky dossier, flashed a smile at the two agents, and departed.

Waverly adopted his favorite lecturer stance, took a brier pipe from his pocket and began to twist the bowl between knobbly fingers.

He said, "There is nothing new in the flying saucer legend. Twelfth-century monks left a record of some great 'fiery ship' which appeared in the skies of France and terrified the peasantry. There have been many such stories through the ages. Wars always result in a bumper crop. For instance—"

He turned the pages of the file.

"—here's a clipping from a Welsh newspaper just after the Boer War. It speaks of 'balls of fire' that appeared in many places in South Wales and, apparently, dropped in persistently at the meetings of the noted evangelist Mrs. Mary Jones. One is even said to have followed her car for miles along winding roads.

"Here's another cutting. It seems that walking along a road near Caerphilly on the night of May 18, 1909, a

Mr. Lithbridge, of Roland Street, Cardiff, saw on the grass a huge tube-shaped craft carrying two men in fur overcoats. When he came in sight' they jabbered together in some unknown tongue, and the machine took off swiftly into the blue."

Solo nodded.

"There were many similar yarns after World War II," he said. "Wasn't a flock of flying saucers supposed to have massed over the Pentagon one night?"

Illya said, "I remember that. A couple of pursuit planes went up after them. They crashed and both pilots were killed."

Waverly polished his brier thoughtfully. "Most of the tales can be dismissed as sheer fantasy—the aftermath of a turkey dinner or a drink too many," he said. "But some of the sightings simply can't be explained away so easily.

"Quite recently a party of Danish scientists were returning by air from viewing an eclipse of the sun in Africa. Suddenly—in broad daylight—some huge flying object appeared out of nowhere and kept pace with their aircraft for miles. They had time to film it with a 16mm camera and to take a series of still photographs before it disappeared as mysteriously as it had come. They saw *something* outside of normal experience. Their statements are here." He tapped the file on the table. "But what did they see, and where did it come from?"

He went to a locker and produced a misshapen lump of something that might have been dirty glass.

"What, gentlemen, do you make of that?"

The two agents examined it. It was quite smooth, dark—almost black—and weighed around ten pounds.

Solo said, "Whatever it is, it's been under intense heat. Some kind of volcanic rock, maybe."

Waverly said, "A Copenhagen newspaperman, not given to sensationalism, got a tip that strange things were happening on Jutland. He went to the island to investigate and heard stories of weird, silent machines which flew at incredible speed and could rise and drop vertically. A farmer took him to the place where he swore he had seen one of the monsters actually taking off. The reporter saw a great circular patch of scorched ground where the very boulders had fused like lava. He brought this piece away as evidence.

"We put our people in Copenhagen onto the matter. Now—well, you have seen the films . . ."

"And Norah Bland died getting them to us," Illya said. "There's not much fantasy about that."

There was a short silence. Then Solo said, "This man Garbridge—who is he?"

Waverly picked up the file and thumbed through it.

"You'll find him in here. He is an Irishman, the black sheep of a fine old army family. A professional soldier, cashiered following an unpleasant business involving the daughter of one of his sergeants. The girl died. That happened in 1938. When he was thrown out of the army he went to live in Denmark and he has been there ever since.

"During the occupation his Irish passport saved him from internment. The Danes suspected him of collaboration with the Germans, but they could never prove it. Oddly, the Germans suspected him of working with the Resistance. They couldn't prove it either. But they were both right. He was a ruthless and diabolically clever double-agent, owing allegiance to only one power."

Illya said softly, "Thrush!"

Spin a globe of the world. Examine every inch of it. You will never find the name of Thrush engraved there. Yet time and again, as you pass your hand over country after country, you will be touching unwittingly on territories dominated by that sinister nation. Those territories are designated by Thrush as Satraps.

Thrush has no geographical boundaries as we understand them. There are self-contained units in various sections of many countries—and these units, these Satraps, owe their allegiance to Thrush alone.

A Satrap may take the form of a manufacturing complex, or a school, or a hospital, or a maze of underground tunnels and caverns, or a department store in the heart of a big city. The Satraps exist as functional parts of the society in which they have been set down. But they have a shadow existence all their own, a secret life in which they dedicate their fanatic loyalty to Thrush.

For Thrush, like other nations, has a national purpose. Thrush's purpose is to dominate the earth.

Thrush has its own structure of authority. At the top is the Council—a group of men and women, all leaders in their various fields and almost universally super-intellects and scientists. They all hold positions of importance in their own countries. But no matter where they live, no matter what their race, creed or color, they pledge their loyalty to Thrush.

They are a renegade handful of brilliant intellects seeing themselves as super-beings whose mission is to dominate the earth. Beneath them, scattered among the Satraps, are their minions . . . the lesser men and women who execute the Council's commands.

At regular intervals the members of the Council meet in the capital city of the organization. The capital city is called Thrush and the entire organization takes its name from it. Like the different Satraps, the capital city is concealed under a specific "cover". But unlike the Satraps, the City of Thrush is mobile. It is shifted constantly from place to place, from country to country, from underground to land to sea to air and back again. It is never allowed to stay in any one place long enough for an enemy to find and destroy it.

The capital city contains all the requisites of government. It has its army, its civil service, its departments and echelons of leadership. Most importantly, it contains the Ultimate Computor. All decisions of the Council are made by this machine, a marvellous, almost infallible organism developed by the brightest minds of Thrush. The Council will collect all information on any subject or project, feed the information to the Ultimate Computor, then follow the plan of action it develops. When Thrush fails it is not through any flaw in the computor. It is through human error or superior force of the enemy.

With fantastic brains, resources, money and power at its command, Thrush is the most deadly threat the world has ever known. It has great armies equipped with the most modern weapons. It has the most advanced methods of communication, transportation, factories, laboratories, and it has an enormous treasury constantly replenished and fattened by legitimate and illegitimate enterprises.

Thrush is not an organization of criminals like the Mafia or Cosa Nostra. It is not a secret agency for any of the powers of the world. It is a supra-nation, led by super-intellects under the guidance of the Ultimate Computor—and it is constantly at war. Thrush has no allies. It has only enemies. Good men or evil men, if you are not a member of Thrush, you are marked to be ruled or destroyed.

Waverly said, "Garbridge is Thrush's Council man directing the Danish and Swedish satraps. There is no doubt at all that his units are behind this 'flying saucer' business. You can imagine what an asset a machine like that would be to Thrush."

"I can see the panic there'd be if a flock of those things suddenly appeared in the sky over New York or London," Solo agreed. "Everybody would think that the Martians were landing."

"Exactly! Defenses would be thrown into chaos for those first few vital hours. We must stop that happening —by destroying the things now, while they are still in the experimental stage."

Waverly's rubbery face lightened. "So far, our reports show, not one machine has been completely successful. Every flight traced has ended in a crash and usually a totally destructive explosion. But that will not necessarily continue. Thrush has some of the best aeronautical brains in the world at its disposal. And they are persistent."

"But where are they making the things?" Solo asked. "A project like that would need a vast factory. Where would they hide it on a small island like Jutland?"

"That," said Waverly, "is what you are going to find out."

# CHAPTER FOUR

THE SEA-WASHED WIND of early morning was blowing on Solo's face as he walked through the Gammel Strand fish market. There was more than a touch of frost in the clean air. He turned into a tall, old-fashioned building and climbed to the third floor.

It took a few minutes to locate the office of Paramount Products A/S, and when he found it there was nobody in the reception room but a blonde girl at the switchboard. She said, "Good day. Did you want somebody?" and rolled big eyes.

Solo said, "We'll take it up after office hours, but right now I want to talk to Mr. Jorgensen. The name's Solo."

The girl said, "Solo," as if it tasted sour. "Have you an appointment?"

"You tell him," Solo said, "I need to see him so badly

39

I came out without my morning coffee. We were at school together and I just remembered about it."

"You went to school?" she asked incredulously. She knocked on an inner door and went in. Reappearing, she held the door wide. She said, "Mr. Solo, Mr. Jorgensen will see you." It sounded like a big favor.

Mr. Jorgensen was the kind of man who spends his time in garden suburbs fiddling with rose trees and crazy paving. He was small and skimpy and short on hair. He wore a black jacket and gray pants. His collar gave his Adam's apple plenty of air and it was fastened with a dark gray tie. He said, "Good day, good day. How can I help you?" He was smiling, but his eyes were cautious.

Solo said, "Mr. Waverly, of your New York branch, asked me to contact you."

The cautious look went out of his eyes. "I heard you might call," he admitted. "What can I do for you?"

Solo said, "I thought I might call on a mutual friend at the Rodehus."

He shook his head. "You would be wasting your time, my friend. The birds have taken flight."

"Where?"

"That we do not know—yet." He smiled again. "There is something else?"

"Yes," Solo said. "I want an armpit gun, somewhere about .32 calibre, and if you have such a thing, a shoulder holster to match. I've got a Luger but it spoils the fit of my clothes and your Copenhagen police are apt to be curious."

"Of course." He pressed a bell on his desk and the switchboard girl appeared.

Mr. Jorgensen said, "A universal wrench, please,

Gütte. Size Two, with five hundred bolts to match. Oh! and Gütte"—he measured Solo with an expert eye—"an adjustable brassiere for the gentleman. I think he takes a Size Forty."

Gütte's blue eyes opened wide. "Oh, Mr. Solo," she said reproachfully; "and you look so virile."

She came back with several boxes and dumped them on the desk. The wrench turned out to be a Mauser 7.65mm, World War I type but in new condition. The bolts were chrome nickel flat nose shells. The soft leather shoulder rig fitted Solo as if it had been custom-tailored.

"Thanks a lot," he said. "I feel fully dressed again."

Gütte said, "Come again for your summer outfit—if you live that long."

Solo walked across town to the Vesterbrogade. In a sidestreet near the skyscraper *Royal Hotel* he pushed open the door of the *Maritza Bar*. The noise hit his ears like a physical blow. The blue haze that passed for air was scented with cigar smoke and *Jul* punch. Solo pushed his way through the crowd to the back of the room where an elderly man, immersed in the sports page of *Politiken,* sat alone at a table.

He was a medium-sized, round-faced man with a convex upper lip and the bridge of his nose flattened like a plank. He wore an olive-green anorak and a misused black homburg was pushed far back on his bald skull.

Jens Johannes O'Flaherty was the son of a Danish farm girl and a wandering Irish horse-coper. He called himself an agent, which covered a multitude of jobs from booth fighting to acting as power behind the throne in a two-bit Central American republic. Filibustering came as natural to him as patent-medicine faking, and his favorite literature was lives of the saints. The bad boys of two continents called him by his first name but according to his lights he was as straight as a billiard cue. One with a slight warp.

When he saw Solo he registered amazement theatrically.

"Napoleon, me errin' son! I thought you was in New York."

"I got in last night," Solo said.

The barman brought two Carlsbergs in long glasses and Solo paid.

O'Flaherty looked at the beer.

" 'Tis a commentary on the decadence of civilization," he soliloquized, "that when I was no older than you a man could go out with five kroner in his pocket and be a monarch of the night. A few ore would buy him an ounce of tobacco the like of which ye would not find in Amalienborg Palace this day, and for no more there was lager like the gods drink on Olympia. Now"—he sighed gustily—"they rob you of three kroner the small bottle."

He nodded, looked Solo in the eye in the Danish fashion, nodded again, tilted back his head and the Carlsberg vanished. He put the glass back on the table and licked his lips.

Solo called the barman. "Same again," he ordered.

"Barrin' miracles, that settles it," said O'Flaherty. "For nothin' less would make you pay for drinks twice runnin' and you shoutin' the first round. Napoleon, you're in trouble."

The lager came and he swirled the bottom of the tall glass delicately.

"Now," he said, settling back comfortably, "perhaps you'll be so accommodatin' as to inform me of the reasons for this peripatetic perambulation around our civic sidewalks, and you just fresh from a weary flight across the oceans of the western world."

Solo said, "Remember the night at Todos los Santos, Jens?"

"Why wouldn't I?" he grinned. "And I with one foot in the grave and the other tryin' to kick the daylights out of them misconcepted Focacci brothers, to say nothin' of me two guns empty and half an inch of Porky Romero's shiv atwixt me fifth and sixth ribs? Sure, Napoleon, when you came through that saloon door and got to work with as pretty a bit of boot work as I ever had the pleasure of witnessin' I give you my word I had begun to misdoubt would Mrs. O'Flaherty's boy see the risin' of another sun. 'Twas my life you gave me without a doubt."

"Fine. Now here's where you can start squaring up."

O'Flaherty said, "Is there a murder in it, then, or just a nice fancy piece of robbery with violence?"

"Neither. All I want is information."

"As to that," he said, " 'tis well known from Callao to Crooked Corners, Wisconsin, that in the matter of disseminatin' elucidation and verbiage Jens Johannes O'-Flaherty is in a class with himself. Would it be Epstein's Theory that's troublin' you, now, or was you wishful of considerin' the finer divagations of the higher pragmatism, with a sideglance at the influence of the moon upon the tides at Langelinie?"

Solo cut straight through the Irish. "Where does Garbridge's mob hang out?"

His bald dome creased like corrugated sheeting.

"Garbridge," he repeated. "There was a Lefty Garstein runnin' a cleaners and pressers protection racket

43

in Akron, Ohio, in '29, and Honky Garside was a torpedo for Hymie Weiss in Chicago, but—"

"Cut it," Solo said. "I'm talking about the top-drawer thug called Garbridge with a swank layout in Holte. He's got a hideout around here and you know where it is."

The creases ironed out and O'Flaherty's face went dead. He gazed over Solo's shoulder into the swirling tobacco haze. He said woodenly, "I never heard of any Garbridge."

"And I never heard of L. B. Johnson. What's the matter? Scared?"

A full minute passed before he answered, and then his voice was cold sober.

"Napoleon," he said, "I have the reputation of being a tough boyo and it's yourself knows the truth of it. In sixty years of roamin' the far corners of the earth I never yet knew what it felt like to drink water and—God between us and harm—I never will.

"I've taken me chances with spiggotty insurrectionists and I've been town marshal of Concho, Arizona, and durin' the late unpleasantness I did me small stint here with Holger Danske to make the Hun feel unwelcome. But I know me limitations. And I'm tellin' you, Napoleon, they consists of drawin' the line at tanglin' with the crazy man you speak of.

"Sure, I'm scared, and ye can make the most of it, but it's yourself I'm scared for. A poor misservice I'd be doin' for the life I owe ye to help you out with the information ye're after. Bad men is one thing, and you and me can handle 'em, but madmen are another. And mad they are, not barrin' Garbridge himself, the blackest hearted devil that ever disgraced the mother that bore him. No, Napoleon, I'll not help ye."

Solo tried to smile, but he didn't feel so good.

"My flesh is creeping like a laddered nylon," he said, "and the icebergs in my bloodstream are giving me sciatica. The trouble is, Jens, I've got to mix it with these boys because the only alternative is a lifetime of slavery for all of us, and I don't seem to have the temperament."

O'Flaherty's glass crashed on the table like a bursting shell, showering lager over his anorak. "By the holy!" he exclaimed. "There's commies in it."

"Worse," Solo confirmed.

"Now why the devil didn't ye say so in the first place?" he demanded. "And I thinkin' you was just bent on a little hellraisin' for the pure delight of it. Is it tryin' to keep me out of the fun you are? Me that made Ireland ring with me desperate deeds while you was no more than a baby in diapers? I take it unkindly of ye, Napoleon, to treat an old man so. Come on, now, and let's be flayin' the hide off of the crazy hellions would side the enemies of the true democracy."

He was on his feet, all set to lead a frontal attack on the hosts of Mideon.

Solo shook his head. "Sorry, Jens. It's a private fight. If you want to help, give me the dope and I swear I'll let you in if I get the okay from the higher-ups."

"That's a promise, mind."

"I'll do my best."

He sighed. "You can do no more. Now I'll just see can the bartender find us a drop of whisky to take the taste of sedition from your mouth whilst I give ye the lowdown."

The address O'Flaherty gave Solo was a narrow-gutted house in a tangle of streets behind Nyhavn. It stood in a cul-de-sac. There was a seamen's slop shop on one corner of the cul-de-sac with a cheap cafe facing it. Solo went into the cafe and bought a beer and a smoked eel on rye bread open sandwich. Sitting at a table by the window, he had a grandstand view of the house he was interested in.

It was a two-story building dating from the early nineteenth century, when they had views about how the poor ought to live. In its first youth it must have been pretty much of an architectural nightmare, and the years had not improved it. One only had to look at the frontage to get a mental picture of peeling wallpaper, louse-infested plaster work and a colony of man-eating rats in the basement. Solo hoped Jens was right. If the major were living there, he would find it a deserved change from the Rodehus.

Solo watched the blistered door for about twenty minutes, which was as long as he could linger over one piece of smorrebrod without the cafe owner becoming suspicious. Nobody went in or out and there was no clue to be had from the long-uncleaned windows. Solo paid his bill and went out.

A few yards along the street he found, as he had hoped, a narrow passage. Slipping in, observed only by a prowling cat, he was able to study the back of the house. The lower regions were cut off from view by a brick wall, in which the builder had thoughtfully inserted a door. Solo tried the lock and felt it give slightly. He pushed gingerly until there was space between door and frame.

All he could see was a small shed, sometime whitewashed, and the beginning of a flagged path. It was enough. On general principles it was an even bet that the path would be short, leading probably to a half-glazed kitchen door. The shed door sagged open, hanging on one hinge. Inside Solo could see the rear wheel of a motorcycle.

It was no use straining the lock. Solo released the pressure and let the door in the wall settle back in place. There was nothing he could do until dark.

It was around eight at night when he returned to the alley. He stopped and listened before getting to work on the lock. The door opened easily and he slipped through into the tiny courtyard.

He flashed the beam of his pencil flashlight around the shed. There was nothing much to see: a broken stove in the rear angle of the walls, a few fruit crates, a collection of empty lager bottles and noisome crusted tins under the window on the house side, and of course the motorcycle, a big Honda. Gasoline fumes dominated the smells, but he could pick out whiffs of mouldy sacking, paint, onions and just plain filth.

He took the Mauser from the shoulder holster, pressed a full clip into the butt and slid the first shell into the chamber. The jacket moved sweetly and easily. He tucked the gun into the waistband of his trousers, leaving the safety catch up.

The path led to a door that was solid and not glass-paneled as he had hoped it might be. There was a window at ground floor level on each side of the door. No light showed from either or from the two on the floor above, but that meant nothing.

Solo took a black rubber sucker from his pocket and

47

pressed it against the window to the right of the house
door. He ran a glass-cutter in a wide circle around the
sucker, tapped gently and then pulled. The circle of
glass came away. He put his hand through the hole,
found the catch and opened the window. No lights went
on. There was no sound from inside the house. He lowered himself gently into the room.

It was unfurnished, which made things easier for
quick and silent action. He moved carefully over the
bare floorboards and into the dark passage beyond.

In the passage he risked another quick flash of his
torch. It showed him the front door, a lot of blank wall
and a narrow staircase with a one-in-two gradient. The
oilcloth on the treads was the first sign of civilization
he had seen and all it did was depress him. When he
was prowling he liked a lot of thick carpet under his
feet.

He made for the staircase, treading as lightly as an
Indian. With his foot on the first tread he listened again.
Then he grasped the handrail and started up.

Something jabbed him in the small of the back and a
voice spoke pleasantly:

"All right, mister. Keep going!"

Feeling a gun sticking into the vertebrae seems to
affect different people different ways. Movie stars, for
instance, just laugh it off—a wisecrack, a double back
flip, and *ping!* another miscreant bites the dust and it's
hey, nonny, and away with the banker's daughter.

But Solo felt that the barrel prodding his spine probably wasn't loaded with blank. He kept right on going.

When they were halfway up a door opened, throwing light onto the landing. A man came out and leaned over the balustrade. He said, "Ole? What's up?"

The man behind Solo said, "We've got company. It got in through the back window."

The room they shepherded Solo into was furnished halfway between an office and a lounge. There was a white wood table with a portable typewriter on it, a bookcase filled with directories and reference books, a couple of shabby armchairs and a sofa to match. A large scale map of Denmark was pinned against one wall, with a calendar flanking it. Light was provided by a bulb depending from a center-fire ceiling fixture. It was all as innocent-looking as a Boy Scout's clubroom.

Lounging against the bookcase was one of the handsomest men Solo had ever seen. He had blue-black hair that came in tight, almost negroid curls, a nose and chin like the boys in cigarette commercials, and big eyes that were almost violet. His six-foot frame was beautifully neat in a sweater, riding breeches and laced knee-boots. Solo wondered where he kept his horse.

He looked up incuriously, then went on filling his pipe from a thin plastic pouch.

The other two men filtered in. The one who had stood on the landing was a stocky, nondescript type, the kind that fills the balcony at the movie theater or the unreserved seats at the football game. He flopped into one of the armchairs and started to make a meal of his nails, shooting sidelong glances at Solo all the time.

The man they called Ole kicked the door shut, came from behind Solo and sat on the edge of the table. Solo took a specially good look at him. He was always more than a little interested in people who stuck guns in his spine.

He was about middle height and weight and he had a face more like a rabbit's than any human face had a right to be. It was crowned with lank blonde hair. His eyes were very pale blue, with a thin darker circle between the iris and the white, and they held the depth of warm human sympathy you are liable to find in a horned toad. He wore a gray flannel suit, tight-waisted, and his shirt was lavender silk. A primrose tie and ultra-fashionable ice-calf shoes completed the outfit. He sat there smiling gently and his right hand pointed a Smith & Wesson .38 police special unwaveringly at Solo's belly.

The handsome man had his pipe going. He took it out of his mouth and asked, "Who is this fellow, Ole?" The creamy voice went with the blue-black curls and the eyes.

Rabbit Face said, "Search me. He came through the window."

Solo said, "A stork brought me. Now it's your turn. You say 'So you won't talk, huh?'"

It didn't get his goat, which was what Solo wanted. He said in the same even tone, "You'll talk before we get through with you. Hold the gun on him, Ole. Here, you, Per—search him."

Without another glance at Solo he crossed to the table, slipped a sheet of paper into the portable and began typing.

Per came out of the chair reluctantly. He looked as if he resented having his meal interrupted. He muttered, "Don't try any funny business," and started to frisk him.

Solo said, "There's a gun in my belt and three hundred kroner or so in my right-hand pants pocket. No letters, no papers, and I don't mark my linen. So get it over with. You give me the creeps."

There was a sudden clatter outside the house. It sounded as if somebody had kicked over the fruit crates in the shed.

Ole said, "Blast! Get his gun, Per, and leave the rest." Without taking his eyes away from Solo he said to the handsome man, "One of us had better get out and see if that row meant anything."

The big boy nodded, pushed his chair back. "You stay with him. Come on, Per." It seemed like Per was the maid-of-all-work.

Solo's spirits lifted. It looked as if the breaks were coming his way at last. With Handsome busy elsewhere he was prepared to tackle Peter Rabbit, gun or no gun.

Ole must have guessed his thoughts. He said quietly, "Ten feet is quite a jump, mister."

"What?"

"I'm trying to tell you I'd probably drill you about three times before you reached me. Honestly, friend, I wouldn't try anything."

With his free hand he fumbled in his jacket pocket and brought out a pack of Queens. "Cigarette?"

"Why not?"

He shook one out of the pack, stuck it between his lips, found a lighter. He removed the butt long enough to say, "Sorry I had to do it this way but you'll see why I don't offer you the pack."

"Sure," Solo said. "Oh, sure." He was getting ready for the fleeting chance he could see coming.

As Ole brought the lighter flame up to the cigarette he dived.

Ole fired once, the slug seared Solo's shoulder, and

then he had him by the ankles. He jerked his feet back and down. His head smacked the flooring, but he didn't drop the gun and he didn't lose his nerve.

As Solo twisted to grab him he lashed out viciously and his heel took a piece out of Solo's ear. The pain and the force of the kick set Solo back on his haunches. In a fraction of a second Ole had squirmed onto his back and Solo saw the gun coming up again.

He lunged forward, threw his whole weight on Ole's gun arm, pinning it. Then he started to work his knee into Ole's midsection while Ole lambasted his groggy ear with his free fist. He looked like a rabbit but he had the guts of a mongoose.

It was too bad the big fellow chose that moment to return.

Solo saw his boot coming a shade too late; he tried to roll with it. Lights exploded inside his skull.

# CHAPTER FIVE

WHEN SOLO CAME TO he was lying on the sofa, looking like a fowl ready for roasting. His arms had been yanked behind him so tightly that his shoulderblades were grinding on each other. The lashing around his wrists had stopped the circulation enough to make his hands feel like boxing gloves. His ankles were tied equally tightly and there were a couple of turns of rope just below the knees. It had all the earmarks of a Rabbit Face job. He had that kind of smooth efficiency.

Solo decided there was no point in struggling. It might do some good to have the men think he was still out. He lay still and took a quick squint through his eyelashes.

Handsome had gone back to the typewriter and Ole was relaxing in one of the chairs. It warmed Solo's heart to note that he had mussed him up more than a little. The gray flannel had lost its chic and the lavender shirt was a ruin.

Per was jittering in the middle of the floor. Solo reckoned his nails would last out maybe half an hour, with care.

A new man had joined the party, a man with the kind of face lady novelists usually mean by saturnine. He could not have been there long, because he was still wearing a duffel coat. He was sitting on the table, talking to Rabbit Face.

Per took his fingers out of his mouth long enough to ask, "How's the time going, Eiler?"

Handsome glanced at a wristwatch. "Nearly eleven." He went on clacking the keys and Solo wished he would stop. His head was splitting.

Per munched some more, flicking suspicious glances from Rabbit Face to the new boy, then back to the big fellow. Suddenly he burst out, "Where the hell's the Boss? He said he'd be here around nine."

Ole grinned cynically. "Probably caught up with a new chick."

"Chick be damned!" Per flung himself into the other chair, lit a cigarette after two attempts. "He said he'd be here at nine and he ought to do what he says. I don't like it. Something's gone wrong."

Ole said, "Don't be a fool. Something's held him up. He won't be long."

Eiler stopped pounding the typewriter; he rested his hands on the table and said quietly, "Control yourself, Per, or I'll give you something to moan about. Nothing's going wrong."

The clacking started again and every thump of the

keys seemed to drive a red-hot hammer into Solo's brain. Involuntarily he groaned.

The man in the coat said, "Your friend there is coming round."

Per jumped to his feet again, his voice quavering like a soprano at a village charity concert.

"Okay, okay," he squealed. "Everything's fine. So what's *he* snooping around for?"

Eiler kicked his chair back. He crossed the room and swung a right to Per's jaw with all his two hundred pounds behind it.

Per folded. His worries were over for awhile.

"Just the same," Rabbit Face said thoughtfully, "he's got something there. Perhaps—"

The coated man broke in: "Listen!"

Somewhere in the recesses of the house a buzzer was purring.

Rabbit Face said, "I'll go." He opened the door. Solo heard him descending the stairs.

Eiler picked up Solo's Mauser, which had been lying on the table. The safety catch snicked as it went up. Despite his poker face Eiler was worried.

The dark man's hand slipped inside his duffel coat and came out holding a black snub-nosed Walther.

Both men were watching the open door like a pair of cats at a mousehole.

There were voices below and then a confused shuffle of feet as several men ascended the staircase.

The footsteps reached the landing. The dark man raised the level of the Walther an inch. His face was taut, set-lipped.

Rabbit Face came in, looking serious. Behind him walked Garbridge and his lovable henchman Charles.

As far as Solo was concerned that was all that was required to round off a nice friendly evening. The jig, he felt, was definitely up.

The major nodded briefly to Eiler and the duffel-coated man, raised his eyebrows at the display of artillery, glanced around the room with the air of an officer inspecting dirty barracks. Lying there trussed like Tutankhamen's mummy, Solo could not be missed.

The amber eyes narrowed. Solo managed a sickly grin.

"A-a-ah!" said Garbridge. "You have company."

Eiler said impatiently, "We'll deal with him. Are the 'copters fixed for Horsens?"

The major said, "We should take off in an hour. Meanwhile, this man is a complication."

"You know him?" Eiler asked.

The major looked surprised. "Yes, indeed. And so would you if you did your homework. Napoleon Solo is the inquisitive young man who has already disrupted several of Thrush's projects. Now, since he has been good enough to put himself into our hands, no doubt we'll be able to persuade him to tell us quite a few things that will be useful."

Eiler laughed unpleasantly. "He'll talk, all right." He went toward the sofa, bunching his fist. Solo braced himself to take it, though he felt in no shape for playing rough games.

Garbridge put a hand out. "Not yet. We have things to discuss. We can deal with Solo at the other place. He's a stubborn fool and breaking him down may be a long job."

"You can say that again," Solo grinned, hoping it sounded more confident than he felt. He had an idea these boys would not draw the line at rubber truncheons. Thrush operatives had something of a reputation as torture aficionados.

Eiler thought for a minute, then turned to Rabbit Face.

"Get him out of here. Bjorn will give you a hand. Take him down to the cellar."

Neither of them looked as if they wanted the job, but Charles pushed forward eagerly. "All right. I'll 'andle 'im."

His gorilla arms coiled around Solo, hoisting him as easily as a child picks up a kitten. Solo tried to butt him, but a short-arm jab dampened his enthusiasm. It rattled his teeth but it didn't put him out. After that he quit struggling. He was not going to provide any more fun for these thugs if he could help it.

Rabbit Face went ahead with a flashlight, and Charles was not too careful how he followed. Solo's head hit the bannisters every second step.

At the foot Rabbit Face opened a door under the staircase. His flashlight beam showed a flight of stone steps.

Charles shifted Solo so that he was tucked under one arm. He extended the other arm for the flashlight.

"All right, chum," he said. "You go on up to the meeting. I can manage by meself."

Rabbit Face grinned. "Don't mess him up too much. I want a crack at him later."

Charles stood listening until he heard the other man reach the upstairs room and close the door. Then he carried Solo slowly down the steps and dumped him quite gently on the concrete floor.

"All right, chum?"

"Never felt better," Solo said dryly.

Charles chuckled.

"Blimey! you ain't 'alf mucked it," he said cryptically.

The beam of his flashlight went in front of him up the steps. Solo was left in darkness that smelled wet and cold.

For a few minutes he just lay still and relaxed as much as the ropes around his wrists and legs would let him. Waves of pain were pulsing through his skull, and his ear, where Peter Rabbit's heel had caught it, was throbbing horribly. The rest of it wasn't so bad, because there was no feeling left in his hands and the ache in his arms was so continuous that he hardly noticed it.

With his cheek resting on the chilly concrete, which seemed to help a little, he lay there and thought. If Charles had left the cellar door unlocked there was more than an even chance of making a getaway. Given a certain amount of time and no interference, getting out of a few ropes is no particular trick—provided the man who does the tying neglects to put a couple of inches of gut or silk around the thumbs. That little bit extra would immobilize Houdini himself.

Solo gave himself a minute or two more, then squirmed around until he found the bottom of the steps. As he started to move, his knees hit some small, hard object that clattered metallically as it shifted, but Solo was too busy to wonder what it was.

Finding the steps in the pitch blackness was not too easy. When he finally made it he had to take time out to recover again. Eventually, using the steps as a fulcrum, he succeeded in getting to his feet.

The next move was to bend forward, working his arms down over his hips until his hands were behind his knees. It hurt plenty, and so did the concrete floor as he levered down into a sitting position.

Solo rested again and then went to work on the hard part, which was bringing his knees up to his chin and working his feet between his arms. He did it at last, and with his hands in front of him again the rest was easy. Rabbit Face or whoever it was had used only simple knots on the wrist tie and Solo had excellent teeth.

When the blood had pounded into his hands sufficiently to make them usable Solo got the lashings off his legs and ankles.

His pencil flashlight was still in his pocket. He sent the thin beam over the floor, looking for the metal thing he had hit with his knees. He hoped it might be a sizeable bolt or some other blunt instrument that would help on the way out if he met with opposition.

It wasn't. It was a squat black automatic pistol. And, as Solo could see by the marks in the dust, it was lying within inches of where the major's plug-ugly had dumped him.

Solo went over and picked it up, examining it carefully. The steel gleamed dully and there was the thinnest film of oil on its surface. The butt was clean and polished. It had not been on that filthy floor long.

There was only one answer. Charles must have left it there.

Solo pressed the button in the heel of the butt and slipped out the magazine. It was fully loaded with 9mm shells.

Ramming the clip home again, Solo began to wonder about Charles. There was that rap on the jaw he had administered. It had jolted Solo more than a little, but even a half-hearted tap from that hamlike fist should have put him to sleep for a week.

Why had he been so anxious to lug Solo down to the cellar himself? And what had he meant by the cryptic crack about "mucking" it?

On the other hand, if he were anxious enough for Solo's welfare to leave him a gun, why hadn't he completed the job by cutting him loose?

Solo gave up. Brooding on problems like that, he figured, was what brought good men into the psychiatric wards. Besides, he had more urgent things to think about. Instinct was telling him forcibly to get out while the going was good, and his flashlight, in sympathy, was ranging the cellar walls for a second exit. Pigheadedness was urging him no less strongly to get upstairs and listen in to the conference on the off-chance of hearing something useful.

The thought of getting into the clutches of the gang up there was not inviting. He had been battered around enough for one evening. He was paid for just that sort of thing—but there was no law that said he had to enjoy it.

Then, for no reason at all, he thought of Norah Bland.

He sighed and started up the steps.

The cellar door swung open when he twisted the handle and he stepped cautiously into the hall. This time he got to the landing undetected, though there was a bad moment when a rickety tread creaked beneath his weight. Keeping close to the wall, he edged along to the room where the meeting was in session.

The major's voice came clearly through the door. He was speaking very slowly, repeating his sentences.

"Come in, Hades. . . . Come in, Hades. . . ."

Something came in, all right. There was a gigantic, shuddering blast that sent Solo staggering, and then he was in the middle of a shower of plaster and dust. Judging by the rumble that followed, the entire front of the house was caving in.

Inside the room, the boys had lost their calm. Solo heard Eiler yell, "Put on the light, why can't you? Switch it on!"

Someone else snarled, "How the hell can I? The fuses have blown!"

The door of the room was wrenched open and the glare of a flashlight blinded Solo. He didn't know who was behind it and he didn't wait to find out. He dropped and fired in one movement. As he squeezed the trigger Rabbit Face shouted, "Solo!"

Then the light went out. A body slumped to the floor.

Solo flattened against the wall near the door. Stabs of flame came out of the blackness. Bullets smacked the opposite wall and ricocheted with a zinging whine.

Then there was silence.

It looked like stalemate. Solo couldn't get in and they couldn't get out. Neither side felt like risking a light that would draw a shot.

The lull could not have lasted more than a few seconds, but it seemed like hours. It was broken by a crash of glass and the major's shout: "The window!"

Guns of different calibres chattered briefly. Then, with a rush, men piled through the door. Solo emptied his gun in the direction of the stairway, never having been trained not to shoot at running birds.

From below came three shots. Then silence again.

Solo lay where he was, pressed against the wall. It was not heroic—but an empty gun makes for prudence.

Footsteps sounded inside the room. The beam of a flashlight danced toward the doorway. It swung around the plaster-carpeted landing, and came to rest on Solo as he got set for a flying tackle.

Illya Kuryakin's voice said mildly, "Mousing?"

# CHAPTER SIX

Solo could see him only as a shadowy figure, but something seemed to tell him that Illya would be just as calm and well-brushed as ever. With his hair full of plaster, his face battered and his clothes ripe for the junkman, Solo felt at a social disadvantage.

"Let's take it up later," he said. "Right now I'm in no shape for an argument. How did you get in here, anyway?"

"Ladder. We've had the place cordoned off for the past twenty minutes. If you hadn't started a shooting match we'd have roped in the bunch of them. Now the Lord knows what Mr. Waverly is going to say. You know how he hates untidiness."

Solo said bitterly, "Untidiness!"

Illya turned his flash back into the room. "See for yourself."

It certainly was not a scene of domestic bliss. Rabbit Face was sprawling near the door with half his head shot away. Eiler, center stage, grinned vacantly at the shattered ceiling with a blue hole between his eyes. A huddle of duffel coat in a pool of blood represented all that was left of the saturnine Bjorn.

The fake bookcase was swung open, revealing the transmitter on which the major had been broadcasting when the explosion had cramped his technique. The major himself, together with Charles and Per, had apparently made a getaway. For some reason Solo felt quite pleased about Per, who hadn't been his idea of a conspirator.

Illya began collecting the fruits of Eiler's typing labors from the table. He said regretfully, "No, Mr. Waverly won't be at all pleased. What on earth were you doing here?"

"I could ask you the same question. I thought you were still in New York."

"More of the old man's duplicity," Illya said. "I came in on the flight after yours to work with Karen. She got a lead on this place early this afternoon."

"A pity you didn't come earlier," Solo said. "You could have saved me a lot of grief."

Mr. Jorgensen came plodding up the stairs. He wore a dark gray fedora square on his head and a shabby brown raincoat. He could have been a minor bank official—only bank clerks don't normally carry sub-machine guns. He said to Solo, "There's another one down in the hall. I doubt if he will last until the ambulance gets here but he is still conscious. He asks for you."

"Did you get the others?"

"One. A small man. A petty crime type, I think."

That would be Per, thought Solo. Unlucky to the last. He said, "All right. We'll come."

At the foot of the stairs handlamps made a pool of light in which a couple of Danes were working on a third man. Halfway down Solo knew it was Charles.

His ugly face was white and glistening with sweat but he managed a grin when he saw Solo.

" 'Ullo, 'Oudini," he wheezed. "I wouldn' . . . be in your shoes . . . w'en the Boss gets . . . 'old of you."

Solo knelt down. His hand closed over Charles' gnarled paw. He said gently, "Who are you?"

Charles said painfully, "Sorry, guv'nor. . . . Did me best. . . . 'E must've rumbled me. . . ."

"Garbridge?"

"Yes." With an effort he managed to half-raise his head. "Don't blame yerself. . . . Fightin' out o' yer clarss. . . ."

His eyes closed. One of the Danes moistened a swab and passed it over the dry lips.

Charles tried again. "You there . . . guv'?"

"I'm here."

"Tell my mob . . . M.I.7 . . . An' 'Oudini . . ." The lips writhed back gamely from yellow broken teeth. ". . . You 'ad me all wrong. . . ."

"I'll see to it," Solo promised. But Charles no longer cared.

After a few hours sleep and a shower Solo showed up at the Paramount Products office in the Gammel Strand. He was wearing a decent suit and fresh linen but there was nothing he could do about his face.

The blonde was still at the switchboard. She said, "Why, Mr. Solo! Did you run into a lamp post?"

"Sweetie pie," he said, "there are times when your humor is scintillating. This isn't one of them. Tell your boss I'm here."

She straightened as if he had slapped her face. Her big eyes got hard. She said, "Go in, please. Mr. Jorgensen is waiting."

There were three of them in the room: Mr. Jorgensen, Illya and Karen. Karen was wearing her student rig, the shabby black sweater and pants and a faded blue anorak.

Mr. Jorgensen wasted no time in preliminaries. He said, "*Gjort Gerning staar ikke tel at aendre.* As you say, 'it is useless to cry for the spilled milk.' Garbridge has disappeared. Some who might have been useful are dead. Now we must see what we have and what we may do next."

"Well, at least we know where they were going," Solo said. "Before you came along and broke up the party they were all set to take off by helicopter for a place called Horsens—if that means anything to you."

"Horsens," said Mr. Jorgensen didactically, "is an industrial town of some thirty-eight thousand people on the east coast of Jutland. There is a factory which makes bicycles and another which makes TV sets, radios and tape recorders. There is also a large meat cooperative. I cannot see why Garbridge should wish to go there."

"I don't know," Solo said. "It's the kind of place Thrush might pick for one of its satraps. The radio and electronic tie-up is interesting."

"But how could they make flying saucers in such a town?" Karen objected. "This would need a huge factory, and everybody would know of it—and talk." She smiled. "Danes cannot help talking."

Illya said, "The factory is not in a town. The films Norah Bland brought back make that very clear. All the activity is in wooded, hilly countryside. But here's the strange thing. Some of the shots show workmen in overalls, and armed guards—but there's not a building, not so much as a sizeable house, in sight."

Karen laughed. "Do you suggest they make the things in the open air—or burrow in the ground like rabbits?"

A sudden bell rang in Solo's brain.

"By God! I believe you've hit it," he said. "Just before the balloon went up Garbridge was trying to make a radio contact. He was calling, 'Come in, Hades. Come in, Hades.'"

Jorgensen repeated, "Hades. The underworld. Of course—an underground factory, like those the Germans used during the war. This makes sense indeed."

"Did they have such factories here in Denmark during the Occupation?"

"They did, though I have not heard of any in Jutland."

Illya said quietly, "But Garbridge was a collaborateur, no? I think we must go to Horsens."

Not far from the Paramount Products building there was a bar that looked as if it had been there for a hundred years. Solo went in, slumped on a chair and ordered a Carlsberg.

With no other customers in sight the barman was disposed to be chatty, but Solo was in no mood for badinage. He was terse and the man went back to polishing the counter with an offended air.

Solo was halfway through his second beer when Gütte

came in. She was wearing a heavy red coat with a cheap fur collar. A scarf was tied peasant-fashion over her blonde curls. She took the seat next to Solo, ordered a Tuborg and fumbled in her bag for cigarettes.

Solo passed her his pack of Queens and put three kroner on the table for the beer.

She threw him a coy look over the top of the glass. She said, "Why, Mr. Solo! This is generosity."

Solo grunted, "Cut out the comedy. You're a big girl now."

She took a long drink, put the glass down, rummaged in her bag again for a lighter. She lit her cigarette, dragged the smoke deep into her lungs, exhaled it through her nostrils in two thin streams. All the time she stared straight ahead.

When she spoke again her tone had changed. She said gently, "Want to talk about it, Napoleon?"

"No, thanks. I'm in no mood for humor. Have another beer."

"I'm not laughing." She swung around in the chair to face him. Her hand came to rest on his. It felt friendly.

She said, "Look, brother. I've been in this business probably longer than you have—a darned sight longer than I care to think about. You think I like doing purl and plain on that damned switchboard? Look!"

She pushed the blonde curls back over her scarf. Her forehead was seared by deep ragged scars, crisscrossed like railroad tracks. She let the hair drop back, slowly peeled off the thin gloves that she wore even in the office and held out her hands. They were charred, fleshless claws.

"Souvenirs of Thrush," she said. "That's when I lost my girlish laughter."

While Solo was trying to control the sickness in his stomach she slid off the chair and patted her hair into place. "Let's get out of here before I start crying into my beer. I want to talk to you."

They walked down to the waterfront and stood looking out over Inderhavn, leaden in the winter sunlight. A big freighter was moving upstream, her black sides streaked with rust. Some of the crew were clustered in the stern, getting their first view of the home port maybe for months. A kid in a thick sweater and white gob cap waved to Gütte. She waved back and the boys whistled on two descending notes. One cupped his hands and shouted something. All they caught was "toni . . . ight". But they could guess the rest.

Gütte said, "I know everything that went on this morning—and last night. It's part of my job to monitor and tape all discussions in the inner office. Napoleon, you must find that factory."

He grinned. "That'll be an easy job. If we only knew where to start looking."

She said, "I do not think you will find the answer in Horsens. That's what I wanted to tell you. I think you should go to Aarhus. There's a man there—an old Resistance fighter." She took an envelope out of her coat pocket. "Here are his name and address. Go and see him. If the Germans had underground factories in Jutland he would have known about them."

Solo said, "Why tell *me?* Why haven't you put it up to Jorgensen?"

She shrugged. "Mr. Jorgensen does not take advice gladly. Besides . . . when I got these"—she touched her scarred forehead—"I was with just such another *traek-lods*—chump—as you. He didn't get back. . . ."

She turned abruptly and headed fast along Havne-gade.

# CHAPTER SEVEN

THE SAS plane touched down at Tirstrup airport within forty-five minutes of leaving Copenhagen. A light snowfall was cutting the dusk as Solo climbed into a cab for the twenty-two mile run into Aarhus.

"Your first visit?" The driver's voice had the lilting Jutland intonation that was almost like the Welsh.

Solo said, "Yes."

"American?"

"Yes."

"You should come here in summer. Biggest Fourth of July celebration outside the United States."

"How come?"

"Don't ask it. All I know, every Fourth of July thousands of Danish-Americans and their families get together up in the Rebild hills—that's about a hundred kilometers from here—and have a real ball. That's quite a sight, mister. Good for business, too." He chuckled reminiscently. "I got a fare once—a Texan—gave me a hundred dollars to take him there and back. For a few bucks more he could of had the cab."

He dropped Solo at *La Tour,* a quiet but excellent motel on the outskirts of Aarhus. He said, "They'll treat you right, here, and the food's wonderful. And if you want to do business in the city or see a little night life, like maybe *Den Blaa Fugl*—that's *The Bluebird* and it's open till 5:00 A.M.— a taxi will get you there in five minutes."

Solo checked in and a black-haired chambermaid piloted him to Cabin Ten. It had twin beds, built-in wardrobes, a bedside table, a writing desk and the inevitable radio. A connecting door led to a pint-sized shower room.

Solo showered, shaved and changed his suit. Then he locked the door, switched on the radio and took a tiny black instrument from his valise. It looked like a Weston exposure meter. He turned the calibrated dial, pressed a button and called softly, "Come in, Jester."

Illya's voice answered: "Jester here."

"What's new in Horsens?"

Illya said, "Not a trace of our friends so far. Karen's still out, looking. But here's a queer thing. Ever hear of a man called Sonder?"

"No."

"He's a top electronics man attached to one of the factories here. And he's missing. Walked out of his office three days ago to attend a conference and disappeared. He never got to the conference. His wife's frantic."

"The police?"

"They're working on it," Illya said, "but so far they haven't come up with anything. No witnesses. Seems nobody saw the man from the minute he stepped out of his office."

Solo said, "Get a picture to me here. Have fun."

He broke contact.

One of the star tourist attractions of Aarhus is Den Gamle By (The Old Town). This collection of town houses and shops, mainly from Aarhus and Aalborg but also from other parts of Denmark, was started almost by chance in 1909 when Dr. Peter Holm moved and re-erected a 1597 merchant's house in the town to accommodate the historical section of the Aarhus National Exhibition. It was the first time in Denmark that an historic town house had been replanted that way.

After the exhibition the house was moved again in 1914 to its present site in the Botanical Gardens, and gradually Holm surrounded it with a unique collection of fifty-three ancient buildings to make a living, inhabited echo of the past. Centuries-old shops and houses line its cobbled streets, there is a post office with its own stamps and postmark, and even a stagecoach that makes its daily run through the town.

As Solo came into the old town from the Vester Alle the thin sprinkling of snow on the high, sloping roofs gave the streets a Christmas-card look. He crossed a wooden bridge over a stream where ducks waddled disconsolately on the ice, and came to the house he sought. The wrought-iron sign over the door announced that the resident was a clockmaker, but the man who answered Solo's knock looked more like a university professor.

He was small and slim in build, and his skin was the

color of old parchment. Thin white hair receded from a high forehead. Almost startlingly blue eyes gazed steadily from behind heavy shell-rimmed glasses. He wore a brown corduroy jacket, a red checkered flannel shirt and gray unpressed pants. His feet were shod in walrus-hide slippers with turned-up points.

He said politely, *"Goddag, Goddag! Hvormed kan jeg tjene Dem?"*

"Mr. Sorensen?"

*"Ja."*

"Do you speak English?"

"I do. But slowly only."

Solo said, "Good. I bring you greetings from Gütte in Copenhagen."

Sorensen said cautiously, "There are many Güttes in Copenhagen, my friend."

"She said you liked this tune." Solo whistled the opening bars of the *Trumpet Voluntary*.

The blue eyes lit up and the parchment face split in a wide smile. "Ah! Gütte." He held the door wide. "Come in, my friend. Welcome!"

The room was low-ceilinged but beautifully proportioned. Old teak furniture gleamed in the light from the plant-cluttered windows. A huge old-fashioned cylindrical stove in one corner radiated almost tropical heat.

"Please sit." Sorensen was plainly delighted to have a visitor. "So how is my lovely Gütte? She is well, yes? But first we must drink." He lit the candle of welcome and set it on the antique table. "You will of course have a beer. Our Jutland beer is very fine. Or perhaps a Cherry Heering?"

"Beer will be fine."

"Good." Sorensen went into the kitchen, came back

with two bottles of Ceres lager and tall glasses shaped like tulips. He opened a box of Obel cigars and placed it near Solo's chair.

They went through the ritual of skaaling. Then Sorensen asked, "You know, of course, the significance of the tune you whistled?"

"I was told you would recognize it."

"It was the—how do you call it?—the theme-tune of the Resistance here in Denmark. This means Gütte did not send you only to bring me *hilsener*, to enquire about my health."

"I'm afraid not." Solo rapidly outlined his mission.

Sorensen listened without interruption. At the end he said, "We know this man Garbridge, of course. We should have taken steps. But he was clever. And the evidence against him was inconclusive. Even in the worst times we did not take a man's life lightly. In his case, perhaps, our tenderness was a mistake.

"As for your flying saucers . . . I have heard the stories. Who has not? But I have seen nothing and I confess I did not believe the tales. In certain circumstances"—he smiled and lifted his glass meaningfully—"men have also told of meeting trolls and goblins."

"But you can't put trolls on film," Solo said. "We have pictures of the saucers. They exist. Our guess is that they are being made in an underground factory somewhere here in Jutland. That's why I'm here."

Sorensen nodded. "One of the old German war factories." He drew on his cigar, frowning. "There was such a place between Aarhus and Horsens. It is possible . . ."

Solo said, "This character Sonder. Do you know him?"

"Sonder? Yes, I have met him. He worked during the Occupation with a communist group. Make no mistake, my friend: our Danish communists were brave and loyal fighters in those days. Sonder was a brilliant man but an idealist—and, like many idealists, dangerous. I should doubt that his disappearance is involuntary. An organization like this Thrush would appeal to his impatience to change the world. He would need little persuasion to join them."

"But what use would he be? You would need a jet expert, not an electronics specialist, for this kind of project."

Sorensen shook his head. "These objects, if we are to believe the reports, fly quite silently. That is part of their terror. But jet aircraft make much noise. I think it more probable that a machine such as a flying saucer would have to utilize magnetic fields of force, possibly tapping the electricity of the ionosphere. Such a thing seems impossible—but in developing that kind of propulsion a man of Sonder's ability and background would be invaluable."

"But the explosions? Our films show the things blowing up."

Sorensen said, "The machines are still in the experimental stage. They may develop defects in flight. In which case, what better way of destroying the evidence than by blowing them up?"

He stood up. "My friend, there is only one way to find out the things we wish to know. Tomorrow, you and I shall inspect the factory. Meanwhile, let us open a couple more bottles of our good beer and be comfortable."

"Tomorrow?" Solo repeated. "But—"

Sorensen pointed cheerfully through the window at the snow-filled sky. "Not even saucers will fly today," he said.

When Solo got back to *La Tour* he found Illya and Karen waiting in his room.

Illya said, "We've drawn a blank in Horsens. Sonder seems to have vanished into thin air, and if Garbridge has been there nobody has seen him. Here's Sonder's mug-shot." He handed Solo a photograph.

It was obviously an official picture, probably taken for the electronics company's personnel records. It showed a man of about fifty-five years of age, thin-faced, clean shaven, with dark hair receding from a high forehead. The eyes staring straight into the camera from behind thick round spectacles were mild, but the mouth was a thin line curving downward at the corners. There were two deep vertical clefts between the eyebrows.

"He looks pretty harmless," Illya said. "What do you suppose has happened to him?"

Solo said, "If my information is right, he's joined up with Thrush of his own free will. Sorensen thinks it's the kind of thing that would appeal to him."

# CHAPTER EIGHT

IT WAS BARELY daylight when Sorensen drove up to
*La Tour* in an ancient covered farm truck. A double-
barreled twelve-bore rested beside the driving seat.
Sorensen was wearing a fisherman's knitted cap, a duffel
coat and heavy gumboots. He pointed to the vehicle and
said, "It does not look elegant, but it rides well. And
where we are going it will attract less comment than a
smart automobile."

He climbed up behind the wheel and Solo got in beside him. Karen and Illya huddled down on a pile of
sacks in the body of the truck. Sorensen said apologetic-
ally, "Had I known a lady was to be with us, I should of
course have made better arrangements."

Karen lit one of her torpedo-like cigars and snuggled
closer to Illya. "Please," she said happily, "do not worry

about it. When I joined this business I stopped being a lady."

"And that," said Illya, "is the most encouraging thing I've heard this morning."

They headed west out of Aarhus along the Herning Highway and were soon looking at snow-covered rolling scenery that reminded Solo of the Sussex downs.

Sorensen said, "This is country that holds many memories. It is the road to Silkeborg. Seven miles outside the town, in the Horbylunde Hills, the poet Kaj Munk was murdered by the Germans for speaking out against them in his pulpit. They shot him down like a dog in a roadside ditch. A stone cross now marks the place."

He waved his free arm expansively. "It is wild country here—all lakes and heather-covered hills. Excellent territory in which to mind one's own business. That, no doubt, is why the Germans chose it for their secret factory. It was certainly not for ease of access or working. Even with slave labor their difficulties were many." He laughed. "We, of course, tried to add to them in our small way."

"What were they making?" Solo asked.

"That," said Sorensen, "is what makes your present search interesting to me. The factory was engaged on rocket research. It was there they made parts for the V2."

"You think Thrush is still using their equipment?" Illya asked.

He shook his head. "I doubt it. We blew in the whole face of the hill. It is difficult to believe that anything can remain."

He swung the wheel. The truck turned onto a rugged minor road and began to climb through thickly wooded country. Through a break in the trees Solo caught a glimpse of a desolate, reed-fringed lake, gray with thick ice.

The truck reduced speed. Sorensen said, "Now we shall see. We are approaching the site of the old factory. I shall not stop, but I think as a precautionary measure you in the back should keep hidden."

A few seconds later Solo exclaimed, "Look!" and pointed to a great white scar that looked as if a giant hand had ripped at the hillside. There were cranes and tackle, a donkey engine, and open cars on a light rail track that disappeared into a black tunnel. A high wire fence cut the property off from the road. Two burly men came out of a concrete blockhouse beside the gate and watched suspiciously as the truck lumbered past.

Sorensen said, "They've turned the place into a chalk mine. You know, these hills are solid limestone."

"You ever see a chalk mine that needed to be protected by an electrified fence?" Solo asked. "Or a blockhouse with machine-gun ports?"

"That had not escaped me, my friend. But can you think of a better 'cover'? Who is going to question such an innocent activity?"

Solo said, "The question is, how are we going to get into the place? That fence won't be easy pickings."

Sorensen chuckled, but made no reply. A few kilometers further along the road he swung the truck into the yard of a small farm and cut the engine. He said, "You can get down now."

A short, stocky man, bearded like a Viking, hurried out of the farmhouse, hand outstretched. He cried, "Velkom! Velkom!" as if he really meant it and, without waiting for an introduction, shook hands vigorously with every member of the party.

Sorensen said, "This is Viggo Jacobsen, an old comrade of the Resistance. He was expecting us, as you see. It would not be wise to return past the quarry with the truck still empty, so Viggo will load it for us. I did not know what we should find, but I take no chances. Now —they are innocent chalk-miners, and we are innocent farmers, eh?"

Viggo roared with laughter. "Knud, we were *always* innocent, *nej?* But come into the house, please. It is cold and a drink would go good. Also, my wife has prepared a little meal."

He led the way into the big, friendly living room. It was already gay with *Jul* decorations. On every picture frame, on every cornice, stood or sat little *nisser*—the gray-coated, red-hooded gnomes who on Christmas Eve bring presents to Danish boys and girls. There were garlands and crowns of fir and red wax candles and long strings of miniature Danish flags. A big straw goat, almost life-size, stood beside the still undecorated Christmas tree.

A lovely woman with hair the color of ripe wheat came from the kitchen, carrying a bowl of steaming *Jul* punch. She put the bowl on the table beside a tray of smorrebrod. Then she said, *"God Dag og Velkom!"* and shook hands.

Viggo said, "This is my wife, Else. *Ak!* she speaks no English, but I can tell you, she cooks good." He roared with laughter again.

Else smiled at him, poured punch into the glasses and indicated the smorrebrod tray. "Please," she said. "Eat."

She said something in Danish to her husband and went out of the room.

Knud Sorensen said, "She is still discreet."

Viggo told Solo, "In the old days she was a nurse in Copenhagen. She was a nurse by day and a saboteur by night. The Gestapo picked her up." His cheerful face darkened. "My friends, they gave her the full treatment. But she did not break. For that reason only, some of us are alive today."

Karen said, "A brave woman."

He made a little bow and raised his glass to her. "As I hear it, Froken, this must be said of you, too."

He turned to Sorensen. "And now, Knud, what is this mystery? Why is it necessary that I must break off my work to load your truck with sacks of straw? And why do you bring these nice people to see me so suddenly?"

"That," said Sorensen, "is not my story. You can speak freely, Mr. Solo. And we shall need Viggo's help."

Once more Solo outlined the events which had led them to this Jutland farm. Viggo listened quietly but with growing excitement. At the end he slapped his knee with a report like a cannon and exclaimed, "Of course! The tunnel!"

Knud asked anxiously, "It is still in order?"

"You shall see." He turned to the others. "When the Germans were here we, too, wanted to see what they were doing. So we made ourselves a tunnel right into the factory. When we had found out what we wanted, we placed a few charges and *boom*—no more factory. But the tunnel was unharmed. It is there yet."

"Good!" Knud stood up and drained the last of his punch. "Let's take a look."

The farmer shrugged into a heavy sheepskin coat. He

went to a bureau, unlocked a drawer and took out a Mauser 9mm automatic and three full clips of ammunition. He put the clips in his left-hand coat pocket and the gun in the right. He looked as happy as a boy going out on his first date.

They stopped in the yard for Sorensen to pick up the scattergun in the truck. Then Viggo led the way into a long, spotlessly clean shed sweet with the breath of the dairy cows standing in their stalls.

At the far end of the shed a square slab was let into the concrete floor. It was so beautifully fitted that the cracks were barely perceptible. Viggo pressed his hand against a tool rack on the wall and the slab swung downward silently, as if counterbalanced. They saw against the blackness of the cavity the first rungs of a steel ladder. Cold air blew up damply.

Viggo produced a flashlight. "I will go first," he said, "to make sure all is well. There are twenty rungs and then you will be on firm ground. You can stand upright. We built well." He was climbing onto the ladder as he spoke. They watched the torchlight go bobbing down and then become stationary.

Sorensen motioned to Solo. "You and your friends go now. I must come last to close the hatch after us."

The air at the bottom of the ladder smelled dank but it was breathable. Viggo said, "As far as I can see, nobody has been along here. The cotton we left is unbroken." He directed the flashlight beam upwards and they could see threads stretched at waist and breast height from wall to wall.

He went on, "Again I shall lead the way. Tread softly and do not speak, for the tunnel conducts sound easily.

And keep your guns ready, for we do not know what we may find at the other end."

Illya took the modified Luger from its shoulder holster and clipped on the butt extension and the magazine that converted it into a sub-machine gun. Solo did the same. Karen slid a shell into the breech of her Walther 7.65mm pistol and gave the barrel a good-luck kiss. Sorensen checked the loads in his shotgun and snapped it shut. Then they moved off cautiously, following the beam of Viggo's torch into the blackness.

After only a few yards the tunnel decreased in height so that they were reduced to crawling on hands and knees. The irregular sides bore in on them to such an extent that at times jagged projections caught and tore at their clothes. It seemed that they had crawled an agonizing mile when suddenly the torch beam snapped off and a warning hiss from Viggo brought them to a stop.

His whispered instruction passed back down the line: "Stay where you are. I am going ahead to investigate."

Waiting motionless in the darkness, they could hear the distant high-pitched whine of some kind of motor and feel a regular pulsation through the ground beneath their hands and feet.

A second whisper came: "All clear." They crawled forward painfully, sometimes bumping into each other in the blackness. The whining sound grew louder and more piercing.

At last the tunnel widened and they could stand erect, every muscle aching with the effort. Groping ahead, Solo's hands came in contact with a solid wall of rock. He heard Sorensen mutter, "Give me your pencil flashlight."

The little white beam danced over the rock face and came to rest on a metal shutter. Sorensen's hand appeared in the circle of light, reaching for a small handle. The torch beam cut out. Very slowly Sorensen began to draw back the shutter.

The first thin thread of light became a sliver, then widened to an inch. The glare stabbed painfully at their eyes, grown used to the darkness. They had to look away. The engine whine was now deafening. It cut into their eardrums like a surgeon's scalpel. The walls of the tunnel seemed to be rocking with the sound.

Solo put his hands over his ears and peered through the opening. The brilliant light caught his face at unnatural angles, giving it the look of something seen in a nightmare. His expression did nothing to temper the illusion. He turned and beckoned to the others to join him.

Sorensen pulled the shutter an inch wider. They crowded together, staring incredulously.

They were looking into a vast workshop that seemed to be lit by a hundred arc lamps. In the center of the floor was a giant circular craft of some dully gleaming metal. It appeared to consist of two thick discs placed one above the other and each of at least a hundred feet in diameter. Centered above, like the boss of a shield, was a squat, dome-shaped conning tower or cabin with narrow, lateral ports. A metal ladder led to an open hatch in the lower disc, through which they could see a lighted interior. From somewhere in the base of the strange craft thick power cables snaked toward a grotesquely shaped generator that was obviously the source of the nerve-shattering sound.

As they watched, Solo and Illya saw two men emerge

from the open hatch. Despite the shapeless overalls and the helmet that obscured much of his head, there was no mistaking the soldierly figure of Major Garbridge. His companion, similarly clad, was a stranger. The two men descended the ladder and stood waiting.

A few seconds later a tractor laden with cylindrical objects approached from the far end of the shop and pulled up beside the monster craft. In comparison, it looked like a child's toy.

Solo attracted the fascinated Sorensen's attention by tugging at his sleeve. He made signs to indicate that they should get back into the tunnel.

When they were sufficiently out of range of the generator to make speech audible, he asked, "Ever seen hydrogen bombs?"

"No," Sorensen said.

"Then go back and take another peek. What that tractor is carrying ain't *knaidlach!*"

# CHAPTER NINE

AFTER THE CHARNEL-HOUSE atmosphere of the tunnel the air in the cow barn tasted like wine. They blinked in the daylight. Solo looked at his watch and held it to his ear to check that it was still ticking. It seemed incredible that the time was still only early afternoon.

Viggo led the way back to the farmhouse. They all looked like scarecrows, but Else scarcely raised an eyebrow. She brought drinks, and said to Viggo in Danish, "Our guests will need a shower and dry clothes." Womanly curiosity seemed not to be her strong point.

Sorensen said, "Well, we have seen it. The saucers exist. What to do now?"

"They not only exist; they're operational," Illya said. "They wouldn't be loading that baby down there with bombs if they hadn't ironed out the bugs. We've got to move fast."

Sorensen said again, "How? What to do?"

Viggo suggested, "A few grenades through the tunnel grille?"

Illya laughed. "They'd have as much effect on that great machine as stroking it with a powder puff."

Solo poured himself a glass of lager. He lifted it to eye-level and watched the streams of bubbles rushing up through the golden liquid. "Explosives are out," he said slowly. "The hydrogen bombs would be armed before they loaded them into the bays. If they went up—goodbye, Jutland! We don't dare take any chances. Besides, we want that machine intact. If we wrecked it now, Mr. Waverly would never forgive us. You know how he likes new toys, Illya."

He studied the bubbles thoughtfully. Then he went on, "I figure we have at least until sunset. They won't take that thing out in daylight." He looked at the others. "Incidentally, how do you suppose they get it out of the workshop?"

Viggo said, "That, I think I can explain. In your country I believe you keep the big missiles in deep silos. The sliding roof is camouflaged to look like the rest of the land. When the Germans were here, they hid and launched their rockets so. And these people are using the old workshops, much enlarged. No doubt the saucer goes out through the top of the hill."

Solo nodded. "You're probably right. How many men did you see in the place?"

Illya said, "Apart from Garbridge and the fellow with him, there was the tractor driver and the gang of six waiting to unload the bombs. Two others were working around the generator. That makes eleven. There may have been others inside the saucer."

"I wonder who the man was with Garbridge," Karen said.

"That was undoubtedly Sonder," Viggo replied. "Both Knud and I recognized him immediately."

Solo finished his drink and took out the black transmitter. "I think it's time to get reinforcements," he announced. He turned the dial and called, "Come in, Paramount."

Gütte's voice answered perkily: *Glaedelig Jul*, Napoleon."

"And a good New Year to you," he grinned. "Now, if you've finished with the pleasantries, see if you can get Mr. Jorgensen to rustle up a few pounds of marzipan with pencils, a crate of pineapples and a jar of London fog."

"Can do. How soon, and where?"

"In an hour, if you can. Hang on." He turned to Viggo. "Who do you know near Silkeborg who can be trusted?"

Viggo said, "One of the old group has a farm just outside. He's safe."

"Good!" Solo spoke again into the transmitter. "Gütte, put the stuff into a jet and have it dropped. I'm putting somebody on to you now to give you the bearings." He handed the little black instrument to the farmer.

There was a rapid exchange in Danish; then Viggo told Solo, "The stuff will be dropped within the hour. I'll go now to collect it. Don't worry about my friend. He does not talk."

He put on his sheepskin coat, waved a hand and went out. A few seconds later they heard a car engine start up.

Karen said, "Marzipan, pencils, pineapples and London fog. The plastic explosive, fuses and grenades I can understand. But why the 'fog'?"

Solo poured another Ceres, held up the glass and pointed to the dancing bubbles.

"When your house is infested with rats," he said, "what's the quickest way of getting rid of them?"

The clock in the living room was striking four when they heard the sound of the car returning. Viggo stamped in, giving the thumbs-up sign.

"No trouble?" Solo asked.

"Nothing. The drop was perfect—right on target. And the roads are clear. I met nobody."

"Good! Then let's get down to cases. The main problem is to put the factory out of business for keeps and, if possible, capture the saucer intact. If we can get Sonder and Garbridge alive, so much the better. But whatever happens they mustn't get away—particularly the gallant major. What happens to the proletariat doesn't matter. They're not important. Understood?"

They nodded.

"Fine! Then here's the plan. I'll go into the tunnel with the 'fog'. You, Illya, will go with Viggo, Knud and Karen in the truck. Park it out of sight somewhere at a safe distance and leave Karen with it as general watchdog. Then the rest of you make your way to the mine entrance and set your charges along the fence and at the blockhouse."

He looked at his wristwatch. "I should be able to get to the workshop end of the tunnel by six o'clock. I'll open the shutter and start spraying at exactly six-oh-five. Set your fuses to detonate at the same time. Then go in and start the rat hunt. Clear?"

"Like crystal," Viggo said. He chuckled. "I shall enjoy the feel of plastic in my hands again. It will be like the old days."

Karen said, "You are a bloodthirsty old ruffian, Herr Jacobsen. It must be the beard."

Illya and Sorensen went out to the car and returned with two heavy cases. Illya grumbled, "Gütte's sent enough grenades for an army corps. She must think we're going up against the Viet Cong."

Viggo produced haversacks from a cupboard and they began to stow the supplies with infinite care. Solo took from one of the cases a long, slim metal canister fitted with a short length of rubber hose that ended in a nozzle. It looked like a streamlined fire extinguisher. He attached a body harness and strapped it on his back. When the packing had been completed and the haversacks distributed, he said, "Synchronize your watches. Our timing is going to be vital."

Viggo could not resist a last touch of the dramatic. He brought out a bottle of akvavit, poured small glasses of the colorless, potent spirit, and handed them round.

"To the destruction of our enemies!" he intoned.

"But be very sure there are no slip-ups," Illya said mordantly.

They went out into the darkness.

Solo stood in the doorway, watching them load into the truck and drive off. Then he closed the door and made his way toward the cow barn.

His progress along the tunnel was more difficult this time. The canister on his back was heavy and cumbersome, and he had to move with extreme caution to avoid the clink of metal on stone. But at last he reached the rock face. The whine of the generator had stopped, but that was a mixed blessing. It meant that the slightest sound might be heard in the workshop on the other side of the barrier.

Solo looked at the luminous dial of his watch. The hands showed 5:55. Very slowly and carefully he unstrapped the body harness and lowered the cylinder to the ground in front of him. Then he switched on his pencil flashlight and made sure of the position of the panel.

He looked at his watch again. 5:57.

The truck, with exhaust muffled and no lights showing, trundled down the road. Sorensen, crouched over the steering wheel, suddenly gave a grunt of satisfaction and swung off the pavement on to the grass verge. The truck jolted along over frozen hillocks and came to rest in the shelter of a clump of trees and high bushes. Knud sighed and sat back.

"So far, so good," he said. "We should be safe here. It is about one kilometer to the gates of the mine. From here we must walk."

He climbed down from his seat, slung two haversacks over his shoulder and tucked his scattergun into the crook of his arm. The others joined him and he said, "I think, now, that Viggo should lead the way, since this is his territory. Do you agree, Illya?"

"Fine," Illya said. "Karen, you stay here on guard. You have your gun and your transmitter?"

"Of course."

"Then good luck."

They moved off in Indian file, Viggo leading and Sorensen bringing up the rear. As they walked they smeared blacking over their faces. After only a few paces Karen could no longer see or hear them. She huddled against the lee side of the truck, wishing miserably that the cutting Arctic wind would abate. She thought with longing of the bottle of akvavit on Viggo's table. A snort or two, she felt, would have kept her warm and relieved the monotony of waiting.

The men kept to the cover of the undergrowth along the side of the road. There was no moon and they dared not risk using a flashlight, but the hard ground made the going fairly easy.

Eventually Viggo stopped and pointed to a light gleaming yellow some two hundred yards away on the far side of the road.

"The blockhouse," he whispered.

They moved on again silently. The light grew bigger, more distinct. They could see that it came from the one high window in the building. There was no sign of movement anywhere along the road.

They went a few more paces. Then Viggo suddenly froze. "Look!"

"The guard," Illya whispered. "I'll take him. You two split up and plant your charges along the fence."

He got down on his belly and began to wriggle over the frozen grass like a snake.

The guard never lived to finish his quiet smoke. A karate chop across the back of his neck felled him before he could utter a sound. Illya dragged the body a few yards away from the building and then swiftly went about the business of setting his charges.

At exactly three minutes past six Solo opened the shutter. He had put on dark glasses to protect himself against the intense glare of the lights in the workshop.

The giant saucer was still on its ramp. The hatch in the lower disc was open, but the ladder had gone. The tractor was standing by, empty. The driver was leaning against its side, chatting with four workmen clad in white overalls. Another group of men stood by the generator. The armored cables had been removed.

Neither Garbridge nor Sonder was in evidence. Solo wondered whether they were inside the saucer. That was a chance he had to take.

At six-five he clipped a respirator over his nose and mouth, slid the rubber hose through the shutter opening and pushed down the lever on the top of the cylinder.

A jet of gas under high pressure screamed into the workshop. The men below looked up, startled. Then their faces cracked in idiotic grins and they began to laugh. It was not natural laughter; the sound had a hysterical quality that after a second became terrifying. They could neither stop nor control it. Their limbs began to twitch. They ran about aimlessly, without direction, as if blind, all the time cackling and hooting with insane mirth.

Sonder and two other men ran from the interior of the saucer and stopped by the hatch, staring incredulously. Then the gas caught them.

One by one, the men sank exhausted to the floor of the workshop and lay there, arms and limbs jerking like the limbs of marionettes. After awhile they were still.

"Sleep tight, babies," Solo said. He opened the shutter to its fullest extent, wriggled through with some difficulty, and dropped into the room.

At exactly five minutes after six Illya pressed the plunger. Sound smashed at his ears, there was a sheet of flame, and the blockhouse disintegrated like a bursting orange. Debris spattered down, a jagged fragment of concrete missing his head only by inches. Answering explosions on either side told him that Viggo and Knud had taken care of the electrified fence.

He jumped to his feet and with his gun ready made for the mine entrance.

A searchlight beam stabbed the darkness and came sweeping toward him. A machine-gun chattered as he dropped flat. Thrown-up, frozen earth hit him painfully in the face. The unseen gunner was uncomfortably accurate in his snap-shooting.

He heard Viggo's heavy Mauser go into action. The light went out abruptly.

Illya got up and ran on. The machine-gun was still firing blindly, swinging in a wide arc. He could see from the stabbing orange tongue of flame that it was positioned just to left of the mine's mouth. He pulled a grenade from his haversack, extracted the pin as he ran, and threw. The machine-gunner lost interest in the proceedings.

There was no more opposition.

When the three men got to the entrance of the mine they found Solo waiting. He said, smiling, "Nice work. True Danish efficiency."

Illya asked, "What about Garbridge and Sonder?"

"Sonder's dead. His dancing was too energetic. He fell off the rim of the saucer and broke his neck."

"And Garbridge?"

"Not a sign of him."

"Ah, well! You can't win 'em all. Let's tell Karen the glad news."

Illya brought the transmitter from inside his tunic, adjusted the dial and called, "Come in, Angel."

There was no reply.

"Odd," he said, frowning.

"Maybe your transmitter isn't working," Solo said. "Try mine."

Illya called again, more urgently: "Angel, come in."

Only the crackle of static answered.

Solo said, "Something's happened. Let's go."

They pounded at top speed back to where they had left the truck.

It was gone.

# CHAPTER TEN

DESPITE HER HEAVY sweaters and duffel coat Karen was
suffering. Her face was becoming a frozen mask and no
amount of stamping and pacing would restore the circulation in her feet. Finally she climbed into the driving
seat of the truck, putting her Walther on the seat beside
her. It would be just as easy to keep a watch on the
road from there as out in the biting wind, she told herself mendaciously.

For greater comfort she wound up the side windows.
That was her big mistake. The comparative warmth
was too much for her. Insidiously, imperceptibly, she
became drowsy. Her eyelids dropped. Even the sound
of the explosions at the mine failed to rouse her completely.

Suddenly there came a blast of cold air as the door
was yanked open. A flashlight shone into her eyes,
blinding her, and a gun barrel jabbed painfully into her
ribs.

Garbridge's voice came viciously: "Move over and don't try anything. Keep your hands in your lap."

The flashlight beam swung over the seat, came to rest on the Walther. Garbridge said, "Give that to me—butt first. And don't attempt heroics."

There was no choice. She handed the weapon to him. "Now move!"

He got behind the wheel, switched on and let in the clutch. The car bounced forward.

"Who the devil are you, and what do you think you're doing?" Karen demanded.

He laughed humorlessly. His foot was hard down on the accelerator and his eyes fixed on the road ahead. He said, "You know perfectly well who I am, and I know exactly what I'm doing. If you sit quietly, like a good girl, you will have a pleasant ride. If you don't, I won't hesitate to kill you. Your friends have caused me enough trouble tonight."

"Where are you taking me?"

"That," he said, "you will find out in due course. Would you like a cigarette? No, of course, you smoke cigars."

"You seem to know a lot about my habits."

"It is my business to know about the opposition."

Karen said: "I *would* like a cigarette."

"You'll find them in my side pocket nearest to you. Matches, too. But again, my dear, don't try anything."

She found the pack. The cigarettes were imported Engish. She drew the smoke into her lungs gracefully.

He said, "Feeling better? Keep the pack; I have plenty."

Karen laughed. "You seem to be taking things pretty calmly, considering that your factory has gone sky-high."

"A temporary setback only. I hope that you will restore the balance."

"How?" she asked, surprised.

He did not answer.

They were on Highway 10 now, and traveling rapidly toward Horsens. Karen decided that as soon as they got on to Sonderbrogade or one of the other main streets she would scream and risk the consequences. Garbridge would hardly be likely to shoot her quite so publicly.

Her hopes were disappointed. On the outskirts of the town Garbridge swung the truck down a side road toward the fjord and turned into the drive leading to a large white house. As they went through the gate, Karen saw an illuminated board reading: SOLLYS MATERNITY HOME.

She said, "No wonder we drew a blank here. Not even your best friend—if you have any—would connect you with tiny babies."

He dropped the truck in front of the house, and said to the uniformed man who came running down the steps, "Take this thing and lose it. Run it into the fjord."

He leaned over and opened the door on Karen's side. "Get out. And don't forget I'm right behind you with the gun."

She obeyed. Garbridge gestured with the Luger. "Up the steps, please. Quickly."

He followed her and opened the door. She found herself in a bright, white-enameled hall with a floor of highly-polished parquet. Bowls of flowers stood on tables of well-oiled teak. A tall Christmas tree twinkled beside the desk marked RECEPTIONIST.

She said, "Cozy."

"We try to make it so," Garbridge said. "This *is* a

maternity home, you know. Though, of course, our doctors and 'patients' are all Thrush nominees."

He waved the Luger again. "Along the hall, please, and into the first room on the right."

The room was furnished as a study. It had wall-to-wall carpeting in a warm rust shade and spun-glass curtains in rich bronze. The center piece was an antique desk as big as a family dining table, which went with a chair that looked like a throne. On the table there were a heavy silver inkstand, a silver paperknife, and a couple of old glass paperweights that were worth several thousand kroner. Chest-high bookcases around the walls bore figurines and vases of the best Royal Copenhagen period.

Garbridge sat at the desk and put the gun in front of him. He pointed to another chair and said, "Sit down, please. Are you hungry?"

"A little," Karen admitted.

He picked up a telephone and said, "Ask Sister Ingrid to bring some refreshments. For two, please."

After a short interval a woman came in, carrying a tray of smorrebrod and a bottle of red wine. She was wearing a nurse's uniform, but she looked as if she had stepped right out of a Pollyanna book. She was small and round and pink-cheeked as a cupie-doll. She had snow-white hair, pulled sedately into a bun beneath her old-fashioned cap, and her blue eyes twinkled merrily behind steel-bowed spectacles.

She put the tray on the desk in front of Garbridge and poured two glasses of wine. She gave Karen a plate and a knife and fork and put one of the glasses before her. Then she stepped back, bobbed a curtsy, and stood waiting for further orders.

Garbridge said, "Thank you, Sister. That will be all ... for the moment."

She smiled understandingly. The point of her little red tongue popped out and circled her lips. Then she curtsied again and went out of the room.

Garbridge pushed the tray toward Karen. It held open sandwiches of smoked eel, hard-boiled egg crowned with caviar, bacon and asparagus tips, beef with beet-root.

He said, "Please help yourself. I am not hungry. I'll drink a glass of wine to keep you company."

She looked at him, puzzled.

"You are an extraordinary man," she said. "This is hardly the kind of treatment I expected."

He shrugged. "We are both in the same line of business. Both professionals. The fortunes of war have put you into my hands. There is no reason why we should not be civilized about it. After all"—he smiled bitterly—"I was once a gentleman."

He rose and walked to the door. "I shall leave you in peace to finish your meal. I must attend to a little urgent business."

As soon as he had closed the door behind him Karen went over to the windows and examined them. They were double-glazed and there were stout steel bars between the panes.

She crossed to the door. As she had expected, it was locked. There was no hope there. She went back to the table and ate a smoked eel sandwich philosophically.

The phone bell shrilled in the Jacobsen farmhouse, cutting in on the discussion of four very worried men. Viggo went to the instrument and took up the receiver.

He gave his name, listened, then exclaimed, "What? Repeat that, please."

He turned and looked to where Solo was sitting. He said, "It's Garbridge. He wants to talk to you."

Illya said incredulously, "You're joking, of course."

Solo took the receiver from Viggo's hand. He snapped, "Who is this?"

There was no mistaking Garbridge's voice. It came loud and clear over the wire. It said, "Solo, listen and don't ask questions. If you interrupt I shall hang up. This is not a discussion. It is an ultimatum.

"Your delightful if impetous Karen is my guest. I give you my word that she is unharmed and is being well treated.

"You have until seven o'clock tomorrow morning to withdraw your men and clear out of the district without further damage to the mine or its contents.

"If you agree, she will be released. If you do not, I give you my word that she will be dead within the day . . . and the manner of her death will not be pleasant. I have an expert in such matters."

The line went dead.

Garbridge replaced his receiver with a satisfied smile and returned to the study. He looked at Karen's empty plate and the depleted tray of sandwiches. "I am glad you ate well," he said. "I am afraid you may yet need all your strength."

He poured another glass of wine for her and resumed his place in the thronelike chair. For a second or two he sat silent, looking at her steadily with those feline amber eyes.

At last he said, "I have been talking to your friend Solo."

"I don't believe it. How could you know where he is?"

He made an impatient gesture. "Do you think U.N. C.L.E. has the only efficient intelligence service? It was not hard to figure out that he would have made the Jacobsens his base of operations.

"But that is beside the point. What concerns you is that I have made him a simple, and, I think, generous offer—your life against my machine. Unfortunately, he is a stubborn man. I have a feeling that he may not accept. In that case I trust I can rely upon you to make one final effort to persuade him." He smiled. "I can assure you that I have no wish to kill you, my dear. I hate the senseless destruction of beauty. But sometimes, alas, there is no other course."

Karen lit one of the cigarettes he had given her. She was glad to see that the hand holding the match was quite steady. She asked slowly, "What good would my death do you?"

"Frankly, none—except the ignoble satisfaction of revenge."

"I am expendable," she pointed out. "A *tarveligt*, run-of-the-mill agent. Can you really believe that whether you kill me or send me back Solo would cease to hunt you down?"

He shook his head. "I do not expect that, nor have I asked it. I am concerned at this moment only with getting my machine safely away. Like yourself—I am expendable." He raised his glass and bowed to her mockingly.

She stubbed out her cigarette in a silver ashtray. "Well, either way, there can be no argument," she said decisively. "I haven't the slightest intention of asking Solo to change his plans."

Garbridge sighed. "That is a pity. But I think you may change your mind."

He picked up the intercom. "Send Sister Ingrid in, please."

"Ah! Sister," he said, when the little plump woman appeared, "I think it is time we showed our young guest some of our facilities. We might begin with the labor ward, perhaps."

"*Ja, ja vist.*" She beamed at Karen, her blue eyes dancing, and held the door wide. "*Vaer saa god. . . .*"

She bustled ahead down the hall, her tiny feet in their low-heeled shoes clacking over the parquet, and pressed the button for the elevator. They descended two floors into the lower basement, a place of stark, unpainted concrete walls and floors and utter, eerie silence.

Happily, the little sister unlocked and flung open a door and pushed Karen through.

"*Se!*" she announced. "*Fodselsstuen!*"

Involuntarily Karen gasped. For the first time she felt thoroughly frightened and terribly alone. She prayed that her terror did not show in her face.

Ceiling, floor and walls of the high chamber were entirely covered by panels of soundproofing material. In the center of the floor, directly under powerful operating lamps massed in batteries, was an iron couch from which dangled thick leather straps to secure chest, waist, legs and arms. There were racks of whips and canes, complicated arrangements of ropes, hooks and pulleys, and strange electrical devices whose sinister purpose the girl dreaded to imagine.

She felt horribly sick and her body was shaking with a trembling she could not control.

"This is Sister Ingrid's domain," Garbridge said. *"Fodselsstuen,* 'the labor ward,' is her own affectionate name for it. Perhaps I should have explained to you earlier that she was once in charge of the special interrogation unit of one of the more unpleasant concentration camps. She took a genuine delight in her work, and it was with great difficulty that Thrush kept her out of Allied hands. She is, of course, quite hopelessly insane."

Karen's legs were giving way. She felt his arm go around her, heard him say quite gently, "You have seen enough." Then she fainted.

When she opened her eyes she was in a room she had never seen. She was lying on a white-enameled iron cot and brandy was trickling down her chin as Garbridge tried to force it between her teeth.

She pushed the glass away and attempted to sit up, but the effort was too much for her. Her head fell back onto the pillow and her eyes closed again. She felt as if she had just come through the crisis of a severe illness.

Garbridge let her rest for a few minutes; then he spoke urgently, harshly. "Karen, be sensible. You have seen the room. You can imagine what the she-devil would do to you. For the last time—speak to Solo."

She turned her head and looked straight into his yellow, white-lashed eyes. Somehow she even managed a smile. She said very slowly and distinctly, "Go to hell."

His expression hardened.

"Very well. You have had your chance. Now, you had better pray."

He walked out of the room. The key turned in the lock.

Karen lay staring at the ceiling. She did not feel heroic. She was drained of emotion. She tried to put out of her mind the horror that she knew she must face in a few short hours. She had no illusion that death would come quickly. The ghastly creature with the twinkling, merry blue eyes would not be robbed of one moment of her fun.

Wearily, she turned on her side. Something hard stabbed against her ribs. She tried to ease her position. The pain persisted.

Then she remembered . . . and thanked the guardian angel who had made Garbridge, in his overconfidence, forget to search her. Her hand went under her sweater and came out clutching the little black transmitter.

# CHAPTER ELEVEN

THE OLD-FASHIONED clock was striking three when Illya and Sorensen walked into the farmhouse living room and took off their heavy jackets.

The two men sitting at the table looked up moodily.

Illya said, "The bombs are disarmed. We placed a couple of charges and blew in enough of the mine entrance to keep out intruders. Any news of Karen?"

Solo spread his hands hopelessly. "We've moved heaven and earth to trace Garbridge's call. No dice. The truck—or what might have been the truck—was seen once, heading toward Silkeborg. And the man who saw it, a farm-hand, was more than half-drunk. He can't tell us a thing. Every policeman and every agent between Aalborg, Esbjerg and Sonderborg is on the job. We've alerted the airports and the harbormasters and coast guard. And nobody's come up with a whisper. I don't have to tell you that Jorgensen's fit to be tied."

"There must be something we can still do," Viggo muttered. "Something we have overlooked."

Illya looked at his watch. "Five after three. Only four hours left. You think he's told her?"

"That's a bet you can play on the nose. He wouldn't—"

High-pitched bleeping stopped him suddenly. He snatched the two-way transmitter from his pocket and tuned in.

A voice came faintly through the amplifier: "Come in, Solo. Come in, Solo."

"*Karen!*" They yelled it simultaneously. Viggo slapped Knud so hard across the shoulder that the little man almost fell.

Solo turned the tuner to full volume. "Are you all right? Where are you?"

They heard her say, "I'm fine—for the moment. I'm in a phony maternity home, the SOLLYS, just inside Horsens. It's on the right, off the main road. I don't know the street."

"Garbridge?"

"He's here." Her voice faltered. "He's got plans for my future."

"I know. How many more in the place?"

"I've only seen two—a kind of butler and a female homicidal maniac. But there must be others. Send the Seventh Cavalry. The Indians are hostile."

Solo said briskly, "We're coming—at a gallop. Tune your transmitter onto the homing beam and leave the rest to us."

Illya, Viggo and Knud were ready and waiting. Illya was slipping a fresh magazine into his Luger and hum-

110

ming some kind of Russian war-song. Solo grabbed up his anorak and headed for the door.

They piled into Viggo's big Volvo, Solo beside the driver and Knud and Illya in the rear seats. Solo put the little transmitter in the glove compartment in front of him. The continuous note of the homing signal sounded loud and clear.

"That," said Viggo, as he let in the clutch, "is the sweetest Christmas carol I ever did hear."

Illya warned soberly, "Don't cheer too soon. We've got a long way to go."

The big headlights cut tunnels of light in the blackness. Snowflakes danced in the beams like a hundred million fireflies and drove against the windshield to make little hillocks at the base. Viggo started the wipers swinging. The engine crooned sweetly, eating up the miles of highway.

Karen felt considerably happier. The talk with Solo had brought back all her confidence. She set the dials to homing, got off the bed and slipped the transmitter between the mattress and the box spring. She tucked the edge of the *dyne* back inside the raised frame of the bedstead and smoothed the surface neatly.

For the first time she was able to examine the room thoroughly. Besides the bed it contained no furniture but a white chest of drawers, a straight-backed chair and a washbasin with chrome-plated taps. There was one big window, set high in the cream-washed wall and draped with bright chintz curtains.

She set the chair below the window, climbed up and looked out. She could see nothing but the darkness of the night and her own dim reflection in the pane. She tried the catch, and to her surprise, it gave. Very gently, she eased the window open. Wind blew cold on her face. She looked down. The ground, illuminated by light from other windows, was a sheer drop far below. She was on the top floor of the house. There was no possible escape in that direction; the best she could hope to get was a broken neck.

Even that, she reflected, would be better and more merciful than the fate that waited her in the "labor ward". If Solo failed to get through, a dive might be the answer. The end at least would be quick and clean.

If this had been the United States, she might have made a rope with blankets and got away. But Danish sleeping habits are different. You can't do much with eiderdown and a sheet in the way of fixing an escape route.

She climbed down from the chair and went over to look at the door. The lock was of the ordinary ward type. She knelt and squinted through the keyhole. The light from the passage shone through clearly. The key had been removed. She felt a sudden hope.

The bulb that hung from the ceiling fixture had a conical parchment shade. With the aid of the chair she detached it and removed the wire stiffener from the rim.

She straightened the wire and twisted it back and forward between her fingers until she had succeeded in breaking off a piece about six inches long. She bent it to the right shape and went back to the door. After several attempts the tongue of the lock snapped back.

Karen opened the door cautiously and listened. In a few seconds, reassured, she slipped through into an empty corridor. The floor, to her relief, was carpeted.

She made her way silently to the head of a stairway and started down.

The staircase formed a square well. Looking over the banisters, Karen saw that she had two more floors to negotiate before reaching the hall. She went forward quickly, keeping close to the wall to avoid the danger of creaking treads.

At the foot of the first flight she stopped to listen again. Footsteps tapped busily on parquet. She looked down and saw Sister Ingrid going into the major's study. She waited until the door had closed behind the squat figure before going on again.

By the time she reached the hall beads of sweat were running down her backbone. The major's door was still shut, but peering around the angle of the wall she could see the uniformed man asleep at the receptionist's desk.

The front door was less than fifty feet away. It was bolted top and bottom and there was a heavy lock of cylinder pattern at breast-height. Even if she got past the watchdog safely it was going to be quite a trick to get the door open without noise.

She took off her shoes and stuffed one into each pocket of her ski-pants. The short stretch of parquet suddenly looked like a limitless sea. She took a deep breath and ran for it.

Her hand was on the top bolt, forcing it back, when a voice snapped, "Leaving us?"

She whipped around, flattening against the door in a useless posture of defense.

Garbridge was standing, Luger in hand, in the doorway of his study. Beside him Sister Ingrid smiled benevolently.

Garbridge was not smiling. His face, grown haggard during the strain of the past hours, was set in an ugly scowl.

"Get her over here," he shouted at the uniformed man, who had stumbled to his feet and was standing apprehensively by his overturned chair. "Hurry up, you dolt. Do you think this is a dormitory?"

The man, still not properly awake, shambled across to Karen, grabbed her by the upper arms and pushed her toward the couple in the doorway.

Garbridge had been drinking; Karen could smell the fumes of whisky. The hand that held the Luger was not quite steady. The amber eyes had lost their cold, hard brightness.

He said thickly, "You never give up, do you? Well, you've asked for it, and by God, you're going to get it. I'm taking no more chances."

He looked at the watchman and jerked his head. "Take her down."

Sister Ingrid said in her little-girl voice, *"Til fodselsstuen?"*

"Where else?"

He turned and went into the study, slamming the door behind him.

Sister Ingrid trotted happily toward the elevator gate. She stood there with her finger on the button, beckoning with the other plump hand for the uniformed man to hurry.

As the elevator door glided open Karen kicked backward viciously, trying to knock the guard's legs from under him. He slipped, but regained his balance quickly. He shifted his grip, forced her arm up and back in a hammer-lock, and almost threw her into the cage of the elevator. Sister Ingrid crooned, "Quietly, quietly, *elskede!* We are going to enjoy ourselves, you and I."

The lift whined downward, came to a stop at the basement level. The door slid open and Sister Ingrid ran ahead, fumbling at the chateleine hanging from her belt for the key of the "labor room". She was murmuring to herself delightedly as she turned the lock.

The man pushed Karen into the room, still holding her firmly. He asked, "Where do you want her?"

"On the operating table, if you please. That's right. That's right. Now, the straps. . . ."

She began to pull the buckles tightly. Thin lines of saliva had begun to dribble from the corners of her tiny rosebud mouth.

The guard's face had turned to the color of old dough. He said shakily, "Do I have to stay?"

"No, no. That would never do. We must be quite alone. Mother's little baby has been naughty, and she must be corrected, you see."

The blue eyes behind the steel-bowed spectacles were quite, quite mad.

# CHAPTER TWELVE

THE VOLVO DECREASED speed. Viggo said, "We're coming into Horsens now. Keep a sharp lookout for the side road."

"In this blizzard," Illya grumbled, "we'll be lucky if we manage to hit the town." There were now almost four inches of snow on the highway and flakes large as kroner pieces were beating onto the windshield, almost obscuring vision.

The steady piping of the homing signal weakened. Solo said, "We're off-beam. We've missed the turn somehow. We'll have to go back."

Viggo swung the car in a U-turn, risking the chance of another vehicle on the road. The signal grew stronger again and after a minute Solo cried, "There!"

They turned down the side road. Illya rolled the

window down and peered out, his eyes slitted against
the snow-filled wind which slashed his face like a knife.
A big sign ahead shone white in the headlights. He
said, "Stop the car. This is it."

Viggo braked, killed the engine and switched off the
headlights. The men got out stiffly, cramped after the
long, cold run.

The gates to the drive were locked. Using his flashlight, Illya found a porter's bell set into one of the pillars. "Shall I ring it?" he asked. "Maybe they'll think
we're expectant mommas."

"Leave it alone," Solo said. "We'll go in over the wall."

"After you!" Illya bowed jauntily, then bent and made
a step with his linked hands.

Solo caught the top of the wall, pulled himself up and
dropped noiselessly to the ground on the other side. The
others followed him, one by one. He whispered, "Get
right onto the drive. The lawn is probably trip-wired."

Not a light showed as they walked up to the house.
The place might have been empty. But the bleep of the
transmitter, now muffled inside Solo's coat, was still
distinct.

They circled to the back of the building. There, too,
all was in darkness. Solo found what looked as if it
ought to have been the door to the kitchen quarters. He
inserted a slim plastic tube into the lock and lit the end
with his pocket lighter. There was a momentary, brilliant
flash and a smell of burning metal. He pressed gently
and the door opened.

His torch beam danced around the room, coming to
rest briefly on an electric range, a refrigerator and a
white wood table. Another door was let into the farther
wall. A thin thread of light showed beneath it.

"Wait," Solo whispered to the others. Taking great care to avoid the table and other obstacles, he crossed the room and listened at the door. There was no sound. He turned the handle. The door let out into a short passage where white jackets hung on hooks. Beyond the passage he could see the entrance to an elevator, and beyond that a section of hall where a gaily decorated Christmas tree towered beside a desk.

He winked the flashlight three times, and the other three joined him.

"All clear, so far," he said. "Now the trick is to find where everybody's hiding."

He drew the Luger from its place under his left arm and slipped the safety catch.

They had gone only a few steps along the passage when the whine of the elevator stopped them in their tracks. They flattened against the wall.

The elevator door opened. A man in uniform stepped out. His face was paper-white. He walked unsteadily toward a big bowl of flowers standing on a side-table. He wrenched the flowers out of the bowl and threw them onto the parquet. Then he put his head over the bowl and was thoroughly, enthusiastically sick.

The jolt of Knud's twin gun barrels in his kidneys brought him upright abruptly. Knud said softly in Danish, "Make one sound and I'll blow your back out. Over here, friend, quickly." He prodded the man toward the passage.

Solo said, "Take him into the kitchen."

He followed them, pushing the door shut behind him. "Now, talk," he said, keeping the flashlight beam full on the man's frightened face. "Where's Garbridge?"

Knud translated, and the man gasped, "In his study, off the hall."

"Alone?"

"Yes, sir."

Solo said, "Viggo, go and take care of him. Don't kill him unless you have to." Then to the man, "How many of you are there?"

Knud listened and said, "He claims that he and some crazy nurse are the only ones left except Garbridge. The rest are gone."

"Ask him about Karen. Where are they holding her?"

The man gabbled almost incoherently, stabbing toward the floor with his finger. Knud's eyes widened comically. He said, *"Hvad?"*

The man stammered again, *"Fodselsstuen! Fodselsstuen!"*

Knud said, "I don't get it. He keeps repeating that she is in the labor ward. He says that's what made him sick."

Illya repeated incredulously, "The labor ward? *Karen?*"

*"Ja, ja! ganske vist."* The man tried frantically to get his meaning home. *"Gestapo! De forstaar? Tortur!"*

"Torture!" Solo didn't need that translated. He said, "Tell him to get us there fast."

With Knud's scattergun still at his back, the man hurried them to the elevator. As the cage opened on the basement floor they heard a girl's agonized scream.

Solo put his pistol to the lock of the door and fired three times. They burst into the room together.

Sister Ingrid rushed toward them. She was holding what looked like a white-hot soldering iron.

Illya shot her between the eyes.

Karen had lapsed into unconsciousness. Looking at

what had been done to her, Solo knew that was just as well.

Illya asked dully, "Is she dead?"

"No, thank God. But she's taken plenty. Stay with her, Illya. I'll send Viggo down with some bandages."

He nodded. "I'll see to her." He started gently to unbuckle the straps that bound her to the couch.

The uniformed man was still cowering under Knud's shotgun. Solo looked at him contemptuously. He asked, "Do you think we could trust him?"

"As far as you could trust a hyena," Knud said. "But there's no fight in him, if that's what you mean."

"That's roughly it. Tell him we need a first-aid kit down here right away. He'll know where they keep the stuff. Tell him to bring it, and fast."

They got back into the elevator and rode up to the ground floor. A jab with the gun barrels sent the man down the corridor on the double. Solo and Knud went along the hall to the major's study.

Garbridge was sitting in his chair, hands on the desk in front of him. A whisky bottle, half empty, and a glass stood near his right hand. Viggo sat facing him across the desk, the Mauser gripped in his big fist.

Garbridge said, "Ah! Solo. I was expecting you. I trust you reached our little Karen in time?"

Knud started toward him, cursing. His shotgun came up, his fingers tightening on the trigger.

Solo grabbed his arm, forcing the gun down. "Easy! Don't let him needle you."

Garbridge raised a hand protestingly. "Indeed, you wrong me, Solo. I never approved of the methods of the late Sister Ingrid—I assume she is 'late'? Yes, I thought

121

so! The impetuous Mr. Kuryakin, no doubt—but there are times when such crudity is inevitable." He shook his head. "You really should have accepted my offer. Now, I fear, we all have our little troubles."

"Your troubles are not going to be little ones," Solo said grimly. "You're through, Garbridge."

"I'm afraid so," he admitted. "You have me over the —er—proverbial barrel. I suppose the only question is where I'll stand trial and on what charges."

"You'll be handed over to the Danish authorities in Copenhagen. After that it's out of my hands."

"I thought so. By the way, would you very much mind if I stood up? Mr. Jacobsen, here, takes his duties very seriously, and I am getting a little cramped."

"Suit yourself—but keep your hands where we can see them."

"Thank you." He got out of the chair and began to pace the room, hands clasped dutifully behind his back.

Solo said, "All right, Viggo. We'll take over. You'll find the porter, or whatever he is, waiting by the elevator. He'll take you to Illya. Karen needs a little help."

"You know, Solo," Garbridge said, "I am genuinely glad you found Karen before it was too late. I was grieved for her."

"I can imagine."

"No, no. I mean it. She was beautiful. Perhaps," he continued musingly, "that is from what all my past— er—mistakes have stemmed. I have loved beauty too much. Human beauty. The beauty of inanimate things. Like these. . . ."

He picked up a Royal Copenhagen vase and ran his fingers caressingly over its smoky-blue surface as though it were a woman's cheek. "They have been my friends, and"—he grinned suddenly—"they will be my friends now!"

Before Solo or Knud could move he had dashed the vase to the carpet. It burst like a bomb, filling the room with clouds of choking, blinding smoke.

Sorensen let go with both barrels of the scattergun. He was too late. When the smoke thinned the major was gone. A black opening gaped where his chair had stood. From somewhere beneath their feet came the roar of a powerful car engine.

Knud cursed and ran toward the door. But Solo stopped him.

"Let him go," he said. "Whatever happens he's finished. Thrush has no time for failures. If we don't pick him up, he's a dead man anyway. Meanwhile, we still have some pieces to pick up around here."

Illya met them in the hall. He looked happier.

Solo asked, "Karen?"

"We've moved her to a room upstairs. Viggo is with her and an ambulance is on its way. She'll be okay. What was the shooting about?"

Solo said ruefully, "Garbridge. He had a neat line in potted smokescreens. And a fast car in the basement. Where's the porter?"

"Long gone. He brought Viggo down to the basement, then while we were busy with Karen, took a powder." He grinned. "Well, here we go again. Let's toss for who does the calling-all-cars bit."

# CHAPTER THIRTEEN

SOLO LOOKED moodily out of the window of the office on the Borgergade at the snow-clad Abbey church. The building, a thirteenth-century Franciscan monastery, was one of Horsens' proudest showpieces. But Solo was not in a state of mind to appreciate its beauty. He was deathly tired, and he had just talked by telephone with Mr. Alexander Waverly in New York.

Perhaps "talked" is the wrong word. He had spent most of the time listening. Waverly was audibly displeased, and he had made good and sure that his chief enforcement agent understood it.

His final words had been, "Mr. Solo, you will find this man Garbridge, and you will find him quickly." Then the line had gone dead.

Not one word of praise or credit for the fact that the

Danish satrap of Thrush had been broken, that the mystery of the flying saucers had been solved and the factory put out of action. The job had not been completed. Garbridge had been allowed to get away.

Not for the first time in his career Solo wondered: What did the man want? What kind of infallible perfection did he expect from ordinary, fallible subordinates?

Within minutes of Garbridge's escape from the maternity home a dragnet had been tightened throughout Jutland, covering roads, harbors and airports. There were mobile police patrols on every highway and every secondary road that the blizzard had left negotiable. Helicopters were squaring the miles of lakeland and forest. But again the major had vanished as smoothly and completely as the stooge in a conjurer's trick cabinet. And they did not know even the type of car in which he had driven out of the underground garage.

Illya came into the office, blowing on his half-frozen fingers. He had been to the hospital to see Karen.

"How is she?" Solo asked.

Illya smiled. "Sitting up and fighting mad. Says she's perfectly fit and resents being treated like a cripple. When I left, she was shouting for her clothes and threatening to walk out in her panties."

"It figures. But how bad is she hurt?"

"Not too much. A couple of nasty burns in awkward places. Some weals. She should be out in a day or two. We got there in time." He flopped into a chair, spraddling his long, thin legs. "What I could do with some sleep!"

Solo nodded. "When I feel like this I sometimes think everything would be all right all over the world if everybody could get a good night's sleep—"

The telephone on the desk shrilled. Solo grabbed the receiver.

He listened, then said, "Where? . . . All right. We're on our way."

Illya sat up. "What was that all about?"

Solo was getting into his anorak. He said, "A Mercedes crashed a roadblock on Highway 18, three kilometers south of Herning. They took a shot at it. It swerved but didn't stop. But a patrol outside Silkeborg found it overturned in a drift. That's where we're going."

They clattered down the stairs and out into the Citroen parked by the curb.

"It's a pity we let Jacobsen and Sorensen go," Illya said, as he slid behind the wheel. "Right now we could have used the Volvo."

Solo said, "What could I do? It's not their fight."

"And cows need regular valeting. I know. I'm an old farming type myself. But it's still a shame."

Solo didn't hear him. He had fallen asleep.

A patrol stopped the car at the intersection of the A13 and A15 about twelve kilometers west of Silkeborg. Illya showed his identity card and asked, "Where's the pileup?"

The policeman said, "A kilometer up the road. The inspector is waiting for you."

"Thank you." Illya jolted Solo with his elbow, not too gently. "Wake up, Goldilocks. Time for your porridge." He turned the nose of the car to the right.

A huddle of men showed up black against the snowy landscape. Beside them was the broken silhouette of an upturned car, its front wheels and hood hidden in a deep drift.

Illya cut the Citroen's engine. As they got out, a policeman wearing inspector's insignia came forward to greet
them.

They shook hands in the formal Danish fashion. Nothing in Denmark, even a funeral, can proceed without
handshakes all round. Then they walked over to the
car.

Solo asked, "Any sign of the driver?"

"No," the inspector said. "As you see, there are bullet
holes in the windshield and in the gas tank, and there
is blood on the back of the front seat. That is how my
men found it. The car was empty."

"Footprints?"

"None. The snow has covered them. But the driver
cannot have got far. It is plain he was wounded in the
shooting at the road block. And even for a well man"—
he swung his arm toward the desolate hills—"it would
not be good conditions."

"You've got men searching?"

The inspector looked hurt. He said, "Of course. This
is first steps, nej? Also there is a helicopter, now the
snow stops."

Illya asked, "He couldn't have made it into Silkeborg?"

"I think that is not likely. Would a wounded man wish
to show himself in the streets? And where would he
hide himself?"

"This character," said Illya bitterly, "could hide himself in a perspex bag."

A young policeman came floundering through the
snow from the direction of a beech wood. He looked
agitated.

The inspector said, "This is one of the searchers. I
think he has news."

The man came up and saluted. He spoke rapidly in Danish. The inspector's face hardened.

He told them, "This is very bad. There is a farm beyond that wood there—a small place run by one old man. My officers have found him shot dead, and his car is gone from the garage. Do you wish to come with me?"

Solo said, "There's not much point. Garbridge wouldn't hang around, once he had transport. How many ways out of the farm are there?"

"One only. A very small road, little more than a track. It bypasses Silkeborg, coming out onto the A15 in the direction of Aarhus."

"But that's crazy," Illya said. "Your patrols are bound to get him."

The inspector nodded. "If he stays with the car, yes. But he may take to the open country again."

"Wounded—and in this weather?"

The policeman spread his hands. "Who can tell what a desperate man will do?"

Solo stared thoughtfully at the wrecked car and then raised his eyes to the snow-covered fields and the wood beyond. He said, "I don't get it. He's back-tracking all the time. Why would he want to do that, unless . . . But that's impossible."

"We're thinking the same thing," Illya said. "Let's get back to the Citroen. Goodbye, inspector."

The little car headed once more toward Silkeborg.

Illya said, "It's crazy, but it's the only thing that makes sense. He's trying to get back to the chalk mine. There's nowhere else for him to go. We'll drive to Jacobsen's place and pick up reinforcements."

Solo objected, "But you blasted the front of the mine

in, and he can't use the tunnel. What can he hope to gain?"

"There may be another way in that we don't know about. That's why we've got to see Jacobsen."

They went into Silkeborg through Herningsvej and cut through the Town Square.

Illya laughed suddenly. "It's a wonder Thrush didn't make this place its headquarters," he said. "Down the road there, in a street with no name, they make all the paper for the Danish banknotes. That could be handy."

They met two more patrols before they got onto the road that led to Jacobsen's farm, but neither had news of the wounded man.

"It looks like the inspector was right," Solo said. "The major's trying to make it overland. *If* he's headed this way."

"I wish him joy," said Illya. "Remember what happened to the Donners. And they had covered wagons."

They found Viggo working in the barn. He listened to their story sceptically.

"A man on foot would not get far in this country," he said. "He had no coat, no hat, and you say he has a bullet in him. No, it is not possible."

"But if he did," Solo insisted, "and if he made it back to the mine—could he get back inside?"

"Another tunnel? Some secret entrance? Perhaps, but I do not know of one."

"Well, there's only one way to find out. We've got to go back there and watch for him."

Viggo sighed gustily. "If you say so, my friend. But if he had the seven-league boots of the fairy tales, he could not have got there yet. So first we shall eat and drink. It will be cold waiting."

They returned to the house. The imperturbable Else served them meatballs swimming in thick brown gravy, with beetroot and sugared potatoes. Solo got the idea that if a regiment marched unexpectedly into the farm she would dish up a meal with just as little fuss. She put bottles of lager beside the plates and poured a glass of akvavit for each man. "The weather is cold," she explained in halting English. For her that was an oration.

It was half-past three when they set out for the mine, and the setting sun was reddening the sky. Leaden clouds were massed ominously, portending a further snowfall, but mercifully the wind had dropped to little more than a stiff, cutting breeze.

Neither human nor animal moved on the dead white waste around them as they plodded along the road. The great tumbled mounds of rock and earth that now completely blocked the mouth of the mine were covered by a deep carpet of snow that rounded and smoothed their outlines. Not a trace of a footprint broke the virgin surface of the hillside and its approaches.

"It looks peaceful enough," Illya said, "but I suppose that if he's around, he would hardly be likely to try to get in at the front door. Much as I hate the thought, I fear we shall have to do a little climbing."

"There is nothing else for it," Viggo agreed. "If there is another way into the mine, it must be on the far side of the slope. Or perhaps on the crest of the hill." He looked at Solo questioningly. "We know this is where the roof-doors of the workshop must be. Could there not also be a smaller entrance—an inspection ladder, perhaps—beside them?"

Solo said, "It sounds feasible. But in these conditions

finding it is going to be quite a trick. It had to be well camouflaged at the best of times. Now we might as well be looking for a grain of icing sugar in a ton of cotton wool."

"True—but at least from the ridge we can keep better observation in case our friend is on his way."

"And freeze to death sooner," Illya said gloomily. He gave an exaggerated shudder, hunching his shoulders to bring the collar of his jacket higher around his ears. "Well, if we must, let's get started. It will be dark in less than an hour."

"We'll split forces," Solo decided. "Viggo, you and Illya work up the left. I'll try to the right. We'll rendezvous at the top and quarter the ground. It's a poor chance, but it's the only one we've got."

They moved off.

The going was even tougher than they had expected. Their feet sank deep in the light, soft snow, often without finding firm hold beneath. They slithered, slipped, and sometimes fell full-length. A loose boulder on which Solo unwarily put his weight sent him skittering ten feet downward, clutching wildly at the yielding drifts.

Then the first shots came, cutting through the snow and sending a shower of rock splinters into his face. There was no cover. All he could do was lie still, fumbling with half-frozen fingers for the gun in his right-hand pocket.

Keeping his head low, he began to wriggle deeper into the snow, like a crab seeking shelter by burying himself in the sand.

Illya called anxiously, "Napoleon! Are you all right?"

"Ecstatic!" he shouted back. "I do this all the time."

Another burst of shots came from above, landing

perilously close. Even in the rapidly failing light the hidden marksman was finding the range.

There was answering fire from Viggo's Mauser.

"Can you see him?" Solo called.

"Not a chance. He's tucked away neatly. Viggo was potting at the muzzle flashes."

Solo raised his head cautiously. The gun on the ridge chattered again. A slug tore through his jacket sleeve and pain seared his right arm. He flattened hurriedly.

Viggo shouted, "He's got a tommygun up there."

"So I noticed," Solo said. "How's your cover?"

"Not too bad. If we kick up a fuss, can you make it over here?"

He had little option. If he stayed where he was, he would either freeze to death or, sooner or later, collect a bullet in the skull. But a quick dash might get him safely to the hollow where Ilya and Viggo were sheltering. He called, "Okay! Start kicking!"

The Luger and Mauser opened up together. Solo got to his feet and scrambled toward the sound. Despite the cold, he was sweating by the time he reached the hollow and dropped down beside Illya. The inside of his sleeve was sticky with blood. He said, "What a lovely way to spend an evening."

"Well, we can't stay here all night," Illya said. "The neighbors would talk. I think it's time we tried a little bluff."

He made a trumpet of his hands and called, "Garbridge! Give up! You don't have a chance."

High above them a thin, stabbing tongue of red flame cut the darkness. Slugs whined and ricocheted unpleasantly. There was no other answer.

"This," Illya observed, "would appear to be what is

meant by stalemate. We can't go up, and he can't come
down. The question is which of us is going to freeze
first."

"He must run out of ammunition soon," Solo said.

"You want to bet?"

"Wait! Something's moving up there." Viggo was staring intently out over the snow, his countryman's eyes
better attuned to the darkness than those of his com-
panions. He raised his pistol, aimed deliberately, and
fired twice.

This time there was no answering burst.

Viggo said contentedly, "I got him."

They waited, then after a few minutes left the hollow
and began to climb. In awhile they could see ahead a
black, still figure sprawled spreadeagled in the snow.

"That," said Illya, "seems to wrap everything up. What
now?"

"We'd better go on and bring him in," Solo said. "He
may only be wounded."

Viggo said, "Not a chance. When they fall like that,
they're dead. Leave him. He'll be there in the morning.
Meanwhile, my friend, the sooner we attend to your
own wound, the better."

"Maybe you're right." Solo turned, and they began the
descent.

Then suddenly it happened.

The whole hillside shuddered as if with an earth-
quake, throwing them off balance so that they had to
grab each other to keep from falling. Intense white light,
brighter than the sun, momentarily blinded them. A
wave of heat seared their faces and melted the thick
snow around their feet as if it had never been. Clouds

of steam rose from the crest of the hill like the plume of an active volcano.

Solo gasped, "Look!"

Silently, incredibly swiftly, the great disc of the flying saucer soared from the hilltop into the black night sky. For a second it hovered, luminously silver, above them; then it canted and made off seaward.

Before a man could have counted five the monstrous machine had diminished in size to no more than a dime seen edgewise. Then, as the three men watched, its course became erratic. It seemed to dance like a crazy firefly.

Illya said, "It's out of control."

The dime edge became a red glow that widened into a brilliant sunburst, making the night like day. A stark pillar of iridiscent light and smoke built like magic into a titanic mushroom.

Viggo said quietly, "Garbridge, *farvel!*"

Wordless, they watched the sinister cloud drift, swirling and curling, out over the Kattegat, its ghastly light slowly dimming.

Then Illya said, "If Garbridge was really piloting that thing, who was the man with the tommygun?"

"The morning will tell us," Viggo responded. He led the way back to the road.

Dawn was breaking when they climbed into Viggo's car to make their last journey to the chalk mine. A thin mist softened the outlines of the leafless trees standing stark against the whiteness of the snow blanket. The big farmer said, as he got behind the wheel, "My friends, I think it will be a fine day."

They halted the car beside the shattered ruin of the blockhouse. A crust of ice crackled under their feet as they tramped across the space where the cranes and trucks stood idle.

"Now, I hope, the place is out of business for good," Viggo said. "It has already cost too many lives."

Solo said, "Don't worry. We'll send along a demolition squad. This time they'll plant the charges inside the workshop."

Heavy walking sticks made their climb to the crest easier. In little more than ten minutes they were staring at the body of the man sprawled face downward in the snow. A sub-machine gun lay near his frozen right hand.

He was wearing a long, padded blue nylon coat and his head was covered by a fur cap. The back of the coat was stained darkly red and punctured by two black holes.

"That explains the bloodstains in the Mercedes," Solo said. "He must have been driving the car."

"But who is he?" Illya asked. "He's too small and too slight to be Garbridge."

"We'll soon know," Viggo said. "Give me a hand here."

With some difficulty they rolled the stiff body onto its back.

Illya said softly, "Well, I'm damned!"

They were looking into the face of the maternity home's general factotum.

"When he skipped out, he must have gone straight to the underground garage," Illya said. "He probably had the car warmed up by the time the major did his disappearing act."

Viggo shook his head wonderingly. "Poor little man! Who would have thought he had so much guts?"

Solo covered the sightless blue eyes with a handkerchief.

# CHAPTER FOURTEEN

Solo looked out of the window of their suite in the *Royal Hotel*. Vesterbrogade, sixteen stories below, was almost deserted. The traffic lights winked WAIT and GO without customers.

He said, "A quarter after four, and it might as well be three in the morning. In fact, I've seen the place livelier in the small hours."

"What else would you expect in Copenhagen on Christmas Eve?" Illya asked. "Everybody's in church. That's the drill: Church, 4:00 P.M. to 5:00 P.M., then home to Christmas dinner. Rice porridge, goose, red cabbage, and all the trimmings. Then everybody lends a hand with the washing-up. After that, the dancing around the tree, and the carols, and the present-giving, and the games. That's the way it goes. And all in the bosom of the family. All but relatives, avaunt!"

"That's nice," Solo said. "If you're in a family. Not so good for the stranger within the gate—like us. Switch on the radio and ring for drinks. Maybe after a couple you'll get to look like Santa Claus."

He walked over to the table and looked again at the dailies lying there.

" 'FIREBALL OVER JUTLAND'," he read aloud. " 'WAS IT A METEOR?' 'LOST SPUTNIK THEORY'. Well, at least we gave them a more original Christmas story than the Jingle Bells bit—even if none of them got near the truth.

"By the way, what about the after-effects? What this lad"—he tapped the front page of *Politiken*—"calls a 'nucleic pillar of smoke'?"

Illya said, "Whatever destroyed the saucer wasn't an atomic explosion. I've been in touch with Department XX3. They say no trace of fallout has been reported anywhere. The cloud dispersed completely about ten miles off Jutland."

"Any wreckage found?"

"Nothing. It—"

"Wait!" Solo grabbed his arm and pointed to the door. The handle was turning gently.

Illya drew his Luger and flattened himself against the wall. Solo, gun in hand, crossed swiftly to the bedroom.

The door opened.

There was a second's pause; then Solo heard Illya gasp, "Well! If it isn't the fairy off the Christmas tree."

Solo stepped back into sight.

"Two!" he echoed delightedly. "And one complete with magic wand."

Karen was lovely in a black cocktail dress under a short Danish mink coat. Her pallor, the only visible evidence of her experience in the "maternity home," accentuated the glory of her red hair. She held up the slim ivory stick on which she had been leaning.

"I'm sorry," she smiled. "It doesn't fire bullets or take pictures or transmit. It's not even a swordstick. I just need a little artificial support, still."

Gütte's dress was in silver lamé, with a scarlet rose tucked into the point of the low-cut bodice. Her ermine wrap might have started life on a rabbit farm, but she wore it like a Birger Christensen exclusive. Her gloves were silver and she carried a little scarlet bag.

She said, *"Glaedelig Jul.* Do you always greet your girlfriends with heavy artillery?" She peeled off the wrap and flung it onto a chair. "When do the drinks arrive?"

"They're on their way," Illya said.

"Good! You want to know why we're here? Simple. The doctors said okay for Karen to travel, so why should she spend *Juleaften* in a hospital? I went and got her. We both know this can be a lonely town for visitors on Christmas Eve, so—*naturligt!*—we come to cheer you up. We shall eat Christmas dinner together."

Solo said, "Great! But shouldn't you be with your own families?"

A shadow passed across Gütte's face, to be superseded at once by a wider smile. "We travel light," she said.

A waiter appeared with a cart bearing bottles, ice and glasses. Illya busied himself with the cocktail shaker. He asked, "You want to eat here? The food is excellent."

"Here? In a hotel?" Gütte looked shocked. "Of course you come to our apartment. You think we have slaved all day for nothing? Right now, I hope, Knud is laying the table."

"Sorensen is there?"

"Of course. Could we leave him out? A bachelor all by himself in that creepy old town of his?" She grinned. "Karen, you think we were wise to leave him alone in the apartment with Lise?"

"Don't worry. They'll cook the dinner first." Karen explained to Solo. "Lise is a ceramic artist. She lives in the apartment below. Her family lives abroad, so we asked her into make up the number. You will like her— but not too much, I hope."

The apartment was in an ancient, pink-brick house in a tiny square tucked away behind Nyhavn. Above the door of the house hung a sheaf of wheat.

"In Denmark we like the birds to have their Christmas, too," Gütte explained. "You think that's crazy?"

They climbed the stairs to the second floor and Gütte turned the key in the apartment door. She and Karen went first into the little hall, turned and suddenly formal, shook hands with the men. They said, *"Glaedelig Jul og velkom!"*

Sorensen appeared in the sitting-room doorway, incongruously domesticated in a woman's frilly apron and waving a basting spoon.

"Come in! Come in!" he shouted. "You must meet the charming Lise. Would you believe it, Karen? She has even provided a marzipan pig. I tell you, she is wonderful."

They shook hands with a pretty, black-haired girl whose skin and eyes hinted Eastern ancestry.

Solo asked, "What's with the pig? I thought goose was the main dish."

She laughed musically. "This is for the *risengrod*— the rice porridge. In families where there are children, it is the custom to hide a single almond in the dish. The one who finds it in his portion wins the marzipan pig. . . . Somehow, it always happens it is the littlest child who finds it."

Illya nodded. "I know. We've played in such joints. The wheel is crooked."

"Please?" She looked puzzled.

"That," said Solo, "was a subtle Russian joke. Ignore it."

The goose, stuffed with apples and prunes, was a masterpiece. There were lager and akvavit and cheeses and pastries and little torpedo-shaped cakes of almond paste. With the coffee Gütte poured a golden liqueur that held the glow of summer suns and filled the room with the fragrance of orange groves.

"This," she told Solo, "can have a devastating effect on one's inhibitions. As they say in England: 'Drink hearty!' "

Later they switched off the electric light, lit the red candles and danced around the tree while the three girls sang the old traditional Christmas songs.

"It is perhaps as well," Illya said, "that Mr. Waverly cannot see us now. I doubt if he would approve of such flagrant sentimentality."

Gütte said, "Come and help me find some nice music." She led Solo over to the record-player. Sorting through discs in the dim glow of the candles took a little time. Gütte put a Henry Mancini LP on the turntable and the orchestra began to give softly with *Moon River*.

Gütte patted the cushions invitingly on the long divan, and put the orange liqueur and glasses within easy reach. "Come," she said. "Now we can be comfortable together."

Somehow, suddenly, they were alone in the room.

Solo took her in his arms. His hand caressed the rounded curve of her cheek.

And outside, in the hall, a telephone shrilled.

Gütte sighed and disengaged herself.

"Don't tell me," she said bitterly. "Your Mr. Waverly chooses the damnedest times. . . ."

---